TREASURE ON THUNDER MOON

By
EDMOND HAMILTON

ARMCHAIR FICTION
PO Box 4369, Medford, Oregon   97501-0168

*For more information about Armchair Books and products, visit our
website at…*

www.armchairfiction.com

Or email us at…

armchairfiction@yahoo.com

SUICIDE QUEST FOR AN OUTER SPACE TREASURE

John North was through as a space pilot and he knew it. He'd been told that at age 37 he was too old to fly anymore. His strength and his reflexes just weren't what they used to be. However, when a fluke opportunity raised its head, he and his aging space veteran friends found themselves hurtling into the void again. But it wasn't aboard a luxury space liner or an interplanetary freighter—no. It was a treasure hunt to Oberon, one of the larger moons orbiting faraway Uranus. Oberon was known as "Thunder Moon," and few men had ever landed on its surface and returned to tell about it. But a small cache of the most valuable substance in the Solar System lay hidden there. Unfortunately, Thunder Moon was the hell of the Solar System. And these men had to brave it in a condemned wreck.

FOR A COMPLETE SECOND NOVEL, TURN TO PAGE 129

CAST OF CHARACTERS

JOHN NORTH

His was an outer space has-been. But could he say no to a pretty face and a chance to return to space in an outdated ship?

ALINE LAUREL

She was a young woman with a lot of money—and she wanted to spend it on an outer space suicide mission.

MIKE CONNOR

This old Irish space dog was as loyal as they came, but his trust in an old "pal" got him a lot more than he bargained for.

NOVA SMITH

She was a "space-girl," an outer space floozy who couldn't be trusted—but without her they would have all been dead.

CHARLIE BERDEAU

Covert and shady business deals were a specialty of this outer space opportunist—but could he be trusted?

PHILIP SYDNEY

He worked for the dreaded "Company." But that gray Company uniform didn't mean he was all bad.

STEENIE

Once one of the best space pilots in the Solar System, his last voyage had left him a space-struck mental wreck,

WHITEY JONES

His experience and massive physical size made him perfect for a long space voyage—even if he did only have one arm.

CHAPTER ONE
Aging Space Pioneers

"MAYBE there's a chance," John North thought desperately. "If they just don't think I'm too old—"

North's small, compact figure, shabby in a frayed black synthe-wool suit, threaded between the docks of towering space liners and through hurrying officials, swaggering young spacemen, and sweating porters, until he reached the impressive offices of the Company.

The operations office of the Interplanetary Metal and Minerals Company, that giant corporation known everywhere as simply "the Company," was a massive block of glittering Chromalloy. Beyond it lay the towering warehouses and docks and cranes that handled the cargoes from other worlds.

John North paused outside the entrance to inspect his reflection in the polished metal wall, earnestly smoothing his worn jacket. His heart sank as he looked at his own image. His dark hair was faintly thin at the temples, his black eyes had tired lines around them, his tanned face looked thin and pinched and old.

"Thirty-seven isn't old," he told himself fiercely. "Even for a spaceman it's not old. I've got to look young, *feel* young…"

But it wasn't easy to feel young, with the hunger he had felt all afternoon gnawing at him, with foreboding of failure gripping him, with his shoulders sagging from twenty years of toil and hardship and heartbreak.

"Straighten up—that's it," North muttered. "Look spruce, alert, efficient. And smile."

Yet he couldn't keep the mechanical smile on his drawn, old-young face as he made his way through busy chromium corridors to the office of the new operations manager. He waited there for what seemed an eternity, fighting the hunger-born dizziness that threatened him. At last he was admitted.

Harker, the new manager, was a gimlet-eyed, tight-mouthed man of forty who sat behind a big desk reading off a materials list to a respectful young secretary. He looked up impatiently when North nervously cleared his throat.

"John North, sir, applying for a berth," North stated, trying to look the picture of a clean-cut efficient spaceman. "I'm a licensed S.O."

"Space Officer, eh?" said Harker. "Well, we can use a few good pilots now on the Jupiter run. Let's see your certificate."

It was the moment North had dreaded. Slowly he handed over the frayed, folded document. His shoulders sagged slightly as he waited.

The manager turned the frayed certificate over, his gimlet eyes starting to read the service-record on its back. He looked up suddenly.

"Thirty-seven years old!" he snapped. He tossed the document onto the desk. "What did you come in here for? Don't you know that the Company never hires a man over twenty-five?"

John North tried hard to keep his mechanical smile. "I could be valuable to the Company, sir. I've had twenty years space experience."

"That's fifteen years too much," answered the manager brutally. "A spaceman's washed out at thirty. He doesn't have the coordination, quickness of reaction or alertness of a younger man. We don't trust our ships to worn-out, middle-aged men who can't meet emergencies."

John North felt his faint hope expire. This new operations manager had the same viewpoint that all the others had had.

The young secretary was looking curiously at North. "You went to space twenty years ago? Why, that was in the earliest days of space travel. Half the planets hadn't even been visited, then."

North nodded dully. "My first voyage was with Mark Carew on his third expedition, in '98."

"And I suppose you think you're entitled to a big job because you were a hero twenty years ago?" asked Harker somewhat hostilely. "That's the trouble with all you older spacemen. You think because you happened to be on the first exploring expeditions, because you got a lot of publicity and hero-worship then, that you all rate captain's grade now."

"But I don't ask for a captain's, berth," North protested. "It needn't even be an officer's post. I'll take any job—a cyc-man, a tube-man, even a deck-hand."

He added in strained appeal, "I need this job, a lot. And space sailing's the only trade I ever learned."

The manager snorted. "Too bad for you, that you didn't learn another trade. Anyway, even if you were young enough, the Company wouldn't want you. The old careless ways of you early spacemen are out these days. Ships are operated scientifically now, with none of the hell raising hit-or-miss tactics of you old-timers. Things have changed."

North bit his lips and looked out of the window to repress his feelings. His tired eyes fixed on the soaring metal shaft that rose in the sunlight beyond the square bulk of the Company's warehouses.

It was the Monument to the Space Pioneers, that marked the spot where Gorham Johnson had returned from the first epochal space voyage years before. North's mind went back to the day when he himself had come back with Carew and landed there, the madly cheering throngs, the sententious speeches.

"Yes," North said dully. "You're right. Things have changed."

HE went out of the building blindly, clutching his useless certificate. Out in the sunlight and bustle of the spaceport, North paused.

The Venus liner whose big cigar-like bulk towered from its dock nearby was making ready for take-off. He could hear the staccato thunder of its tubes being tested. Passengers and porters and gray-jacketed Company officers were hurrying toward the ship. A few bewildered Venusians, white-skinned, handsome men, and one or two solemn native red Martians were in the throng. A band was beginning to play a gay, lilting tune.

North could remember when this had all been a bare field, twenty years ago. There had been nothing here then but the ramshackle hangar in which a score of eager young men had worked with crippled, indomitable Mark Carew to prepare an absurdly small and clumsy ship for the great voyage that was to add Saturn and Uranus and Neptune to the list of visited planets.

That was his trouble, North thought bitterly. He was always living in the past, the times twenty years ago when the world was young and the sun was bright, and all Earth was cheering him and his friends to new pioneering exploits.

"I've got to forget all that," he told himself heavily. "I've got to quit brooding on the past. But what am I going to do?"

He hated to go back to the shabby rooming house over on Killiston Avenue. Old Peters and Whitey and the others were hoping so fervently that he'd be able to get a berth today. They all needed the money so badly.

He shrugged wearily. They'd have to learn the bad news some time. He plodded off the spaceport, his slight, shabby figure unnoticed amid the excited, gay throng that had gathered to witness the take-off of the liner.

Killiston Avenue was part of the maze of shabby streets around the spaceport. Its drab spacemen's lodging houses, drinking joints and cheap restaurants huddled like disreputable dwarfs under the shadow of the Company warehouses. North turned in at his own lodging house and tiredly climbed the dark stairs to the dusty garret, which he and his comrades had shared for six months.

North found some of the others already there. Old Peters was there, of course, sitting in his makeshift wheel chair and peering across the huddled roofs at the thunderous take-off of the Venus liner. He turned his white head.

"That you, Johnny?" he shrilled, his faded eyes peering. "I was just watchin' that liner blast off. Sloppiest takeoff I ever saw."

The old man quavered on. "Cursed if these young spacemen don't get worse every day. You ought to have seen the landin' the Mars mail-boat made this mornin'.

Why, when I was rocketin', anyone who made a landin' like that would have been kicked off the spaceport."

North assented absently. He was used to old Peters. The old man had not been in a ship for fifteen years, but still never tired of dwelling interminably on the old days.

"We wouldn't have stood for such spacemanship," he grumbled on.

North turned. Steenie was coming up to him. Steenie was forty-three, but he had the smooth face and bright blue eyes of a boy of fourteen.

"Do we take off again tomorrow, John?" he asked North guardedly.

"Not tomorrow, Steenie," North answered gently. "Maybe the next day."

And Steenie went back to his chair in the corner and sat smiling vacantly at them. He had smiled that way for years, ever since he had come home from Wenzi's last voyage, a space-struck mental wreck.

JAN DORAK came up to North. A dark, heavy, stolid ex-spaceman, he looked inquiringly at North's drawn face.

"Any luck, Johnny? The new Company manager—"

"Is like all the rest," North answered wearily. "I'm too old."

The others were drifting in—Hansen and Connor and big Whitey Jones. They had heard his words.

"Never mind, they'll have to call us in someday soon," muttered stocky Lars Hansen confidently. "They'll find out they need us old-timers."

"And anyway, I got a little job today and we'll eat tonight," declared Mike Connor. "Look, fellows—grub and synthe-beer for everybody."

Connor's battered, merry red face was carefree as always as he showed his packages. Connor never had worried about anything, even as Carew's third officer on that disaster-ridden second voyage long ago.

But big Whitey Jones, a shock-headed blond giant of forty, slapped North's back sympathetically with his left arm. Whitey's right sleeve hung empty and had hung that way since a tube-explosion years ago on Wenzi's ship.

"Too damned bad about the new operations manager, Johnny," he rumbled. "I was hoping he'd give you a break."

"Company rules don't change, it seems," North muttered. "A man over twenty-five hasn't a chance to be signed on."

"Hell take the Company!" growled Whitey. "As if you weren't a better spaceman than the half-baked kids they've got running their tubs."

North made no answer. What was the use of going over all that again? The others were blind to the changes that had taken place. They still thought of themselves as the pioneering young spacemen who had sailed with Johnson and Carew and Wenzi and the other great first explorers who had opened up the spaceways in their epochal first voyages to other planets.

But all that had been a generation ago. Everything had changed, since then. Interplanetary navigation had mushroomed from that precarious beginning into a vast, profitable trade. The rush of ambitious Earthmen to other worlds, the scramble for valuable metals and minerals on foreign planets, had caused space shipping to expand with incredible rapidity.

And in that explosive expansion the early space pioneers had been forgotten. They had been famous for a short while—but fame was ephemeral in these swift-moving times. And very many of them had died from the hardships of the early voyages in unsafe, ill-equipped, primitive ships. The great Gorham Johnson, the first space voyager of all, had died in his third voyage off Jupiter. Mark Carew, his famous successor, had gone two voyages later. Wenzi hadn't long survived his pioneering trip to Pluto. From ray-burns or internal injuries or weakened hearts, the space pioneers had dwindled away.

And those who survived were nearly all in straitened circumstances. That had been more or less inevitable. They had been spacemen, their only interest the pioneering of space travel. They therefore reaped no riches from the worlds they opened up. It had been the prospectors, and speculators and promoters who came after them, who eagerly staked claims to every valuable metal deposit on the planets, who reaped the reward. And the richest reward of all went finally to the astute Earth financiers who formed the giant Interplanetary Metals and Minerals Company, which bought or otherwise absorbed its smaller competitors until it dominated all interplanetary shipping and sucked profits from mines on every world.

Aging, poverty-stricken, deemed unfit now for the space sailing that was their only trade, this dwindling remnant of the space pioneers had clung together. By pooling their scanty earnings at odd jobs, they had kept alive and hoped for a chance to get to space again. But now the last hope of John North and his comrades seemed definitely ended.

"It's a damned shame, for the Company to keep you earthbound," Whitey Jones repeated. "Just because you're a few years older than a boy."

"They'll be asking us to come back some day," affirmed Hansen dogmatically. "They'll find they can't do without the old-timers."

"What's keeping that crazy Connor?" demanded old Peters querulously in his shrill voice. "I'm hungry and I want my supper."

"Keep your shirt on," came Connor's blithe voice. The battered ex-officer was putting cracked dishes on the table. "Come and get it…"

They ate hungrily in silence, and then opened the synthetic beer. A faint glow lighted the shabby company as they sat over the glasses, and talked the latest space-gossip, of ships reported missing, of a record run from Mercury, of the Company's latest financial piracy on Jupiter.

THE talk shifted inevitably back to the old days, as it always seemed to do. "I remember when—" "Say, do you remember that time when—" Old names of a generation ago passed freely back and forth. Old Peters crushed down any and all opposition to his shrill, authoritative pronouncements.

John North listened tonight with a sense of gray futility. He knew that they were all just trying to convince themselves that they were still of importance, trying somehow to recapture a little of that lost glory of the past, of youth. But tonight he could not fall in with it.

Whitey turned from a hot argument with Connor to ask him, "Johnny, this crazy Irishman says that Carew could have made Pluto if he'd pushed on in that third voyage. I say he's cuckoo. What do you think?"

North answered bitterly. "I think we're all ghosts, arguing over shadows."

They stared at him amazedly. But the bitterness that North had felt all afternoon was now breaking its bounds.

"What good does all this talk about the past do us? What difference does it make what we did twenty years ago? The world's forgotten all that. And we'd better forget it. We'd better forget all about space-sailing, and try something else…"

Whitey answered bewilderedly. "But we don't know anything else but space-sailing."

"We can be gardeners, laborers, anything," North flared, getting to his feet. "It'd be better than always living in a forgotten past."

Then he felt swift contrition as he saw Peters' blinking stare, the faint distress in Steenie's vacant eyes, the heartsickness in the faces of Whitey and the others.

"I'm sorry, boys," North muttered, turning away. "Just blew my tubes, I guess. I'm going out for a breath of fresh air."

He flung open the door, then stopped short. Outside the door stood a girl in a smart white synthesilk dress, who had just been about to knock on their door.

She uttered a little breathless exclamation of surprise. "You startled me—"

North eyed her. She was young, tall but with a faint awkwardness of immaturity that somehow had a charm. He got an impression of dark hair, candid brown eyes and parted red lips.

"Is this where these men live?" she asked him earnestly, taking a pad out and reading a list of names. "Michael Connor, John North—"

"Yes, this is our residence," North replied ironically. "To just what do we owe the honor of this visit?"

He thought he understood, now. This girl was another of the social workers who from time to time had tried to get their little group to accept government charity.

Charity, to those who had blazed the trail of empire across a billion miles of space, to those who had opened up worlds…

CHAPTER TWO
Uranian Treasure

THE girl seemed to sense the hostility behind North's tight face, for a certain embarrassment showed in her manner.

"My name is Aline Laurel," she said hesitantly.

"And I'm John North," he said flatly. "Just what do you want with us? I'm going out."

Connor, always inextinguishably gallant, came forward to reprove him. "For shame, Johnny, is that the welcome to give the most gracious vision that's ever brightened this dusty hole?" The Irishman made a grandiloquent gesture. "Step inside, miss, and pay no heed to this fellow."

Aline Laurel came in hesitantly. That faint awkwardness of her willow-tall figure made her seem younger than North had first thought.

He saw the look of distress in her eyes as she glanced around the dusty garret and then at the shabby, aging men who had risen from the table. Then she looked more closely at Connor's frog-like red face.

"You would be Mike Connor; wouldn't you?" she asked eagerly. "I thought so. Years ago, I heard my father talk of you."

Connor scratched his baldhead puzzledly. "Your father, miss?"

"His name was Thorn Laurel," she said. "Do you remember him?"

"Why, of course," Connor exclaimed. "He was Carew's chief navigator, back on the old *Space Dream.*"

"That's right, I remember him," Whitey Jones nodded. "A big, quiet fellow. Let's see, didn't he get killed out around Uranus in '99?"

Aline nodded gravely. "Yes. I was a little girl then."

"Thorn Laurel's daughter!" exclaimed Connor. "Why, say, that makes you one of us. Hansen, get a chair and dust it off."

North saw that his comrades were eagerly warming to the girl. And his own first hostility had faded away.

"I'm sorry for my...uh...rudeness," he told her. "I thought—"

"You thought I was an outsider," Aline said, smiling gravely.

Connor named off the other men, one by one, and they nodded almost shyly to the girl who seemed so out of place in this shabby company.

"You're forgettin' me!" came Peters' shrill, outraged protest.

Connor grinned. "The old rascal in the wheel-chair is all that's left of Jason Peters, Johnson's head cyc-man."

"Johnson? Gorham Johnson?" echoed the girl incredulously. You sailed with *him?*"

"That I did, young lady," shrilled the oldster proudly. "Ain't nobody else on Earth can say that, now. I'm the last of 'em all."

Aline's eyes were shining. "Why, I know almost all you men, by name. You—you're history..."

North shrugged. "We're ancient history, to the rest of the world."

"I remember now about your father," Whitey Jones was saying in his deep voice to the girl. "He died out there at

Uranus from injuries he got trying to find the levium deposit on the moon Oberon."

"Aye, I remember now too," Connor agreed. "He was only one of a lot of fine men that lost their lives over that lying myth of levium treasure on Thunder Moon."

"That levium wasn't a myth," Aline said earnestly. "My father found it."

They stared at her amazedly. North voiced their incredulity.

"But the System would have rung with it if he had. A deposit of levium such as the stories told of would be worth a billion. You mean to say your father brought it back secretly—"

Aline shook her dark head. "No, father didn't bring back the levium from Oberon. He barely got back himself, in dying condition. But he did locate that levium deposit there. I know that."

SHE delved into her bag and brought out a scrap of time-yellowed paper that she carefully unfolded.

"My father wrote this when he lay dying," she said. "He gave it to my mother. She kept it all these years, until she died recently."

North read aloud the few scrawled lines of jerky writing.

"Levium deposit in west one of three crater-peaks rising from Flaming Ocean. Landing possible only on basalt plateau near spear-shaped bay on south coast. Use double anti-heat equipment. Cross to peaks in stone raft. Look out for Fieries."

"What did he mean by the Fieries?" Connor asked, scratching his head.

"There's stories of life on that volcanic moon," said Whitey. "Weird living creatures that can stand the terrific heat. He may have meant them."

North said dubiously, "The whole thing's not very clear. Your father may have been delirious. The few men who ever came back from Thunder Moon were all half-mad from their experience in the hellish place."

"Yes," muttered Hansen. "That's why that devil's satellite is still almost unexplored. Anyway, nobody believes in the story of levium there now."

"My father had this in his pocket when he came back," Aline Laurel said gravely, taking something from her bag.

It was a little lead glass vial. In it was a tiny grain of mineral that glowed with a frosty, alluring blue brilliance. The shining grain did not lie in the bottom of the vial but at its *top*, pressing upward against the cork.

"Levium..." gasped Connor. "The queerest, scarcest mineral in the universe. Why, that tiny grain alone must be worth a hundred dollars."

They all stared with intense interest.

They had all heard of levium, though few of them had ever seen any. Only a few grains of it had ever been found. It was indeed the rarest, strangest and most elusive substance in the universe.

Levium was an element whose gravitational polarity was *reversed*. It repelled other matter, instead of attracting it. A piece of levium that was dropped would not fall to the ground—it would fly up into space.

It was supposed that the element had had its origin long ago in the deep interior of the Sun, the titanic electric charge of the outer solar orb operating to reverse the normal charges of the sub-electronic particles of this element, thus reversing its gravitational polarity. The convulsion of the Sun that long ago had formed the planets had spewed forth small masses of levium along with the other erupted elements.

Most of the planetary levium, of course, had vanished. It could not exist a moment on the surface of any world, since it would simply fly off into the void. But a few grains of it had been found trapped inside planetary crusts, and there had been persistent rumors of bigger deposits.

"There was more of it in the vial than this grain," Aline told them. "I sold the rest recently to get funds for my expedition."

"Your expedition?" North echoed. "You're not thinking of sending a party to Thunder Moon to hunt for that levium deposit?"

"I'm going *with* a party to Oberon to get it," she corrected him. "That's why I hunted down all of you men, my father's old comrades. I want you to go with me after the levium."

The proposal was so startling that John North was stunned to silence for a moment. But Connor uttered a gleeful shout.

"Glory be, a chance for us to get to space again. Miss, you've brought us the best news we ever had!"

The others' faces showed their excitement. "Didn't I keep telling you we'd be needed again some day?" Hansen cried exultantly.

"But I don't understand why you would want a lot of old-timers like us for such a venture," big Whitey was saying puzzledly to the girl.

"Because you *are* old-timers," Aline Laurel answered earnestly. "I know you're the finest spacemen that ever were, you pioneers whom the world has forgotten. And I felt you'd join me in this because it would be a chance to help all the other forgotten space pioneers, the scattered ones who are sick and crippled and penniless, and can't help themselves any more."

SHE continued in eager explanation. "That levium deposit would be worth millions if we could get it. We'd all share in it as partners, but also I planned to use a share of the money to help all the sick, helpless, old-time spacemen who are left. I know that's what my father would want."

John North felt a lump in his throat. He knew what such help would mean to his disabled, scattered former comrades.

"You're rather fine, Miss Laurel," he told her with deep feeling. "I wish to Heaven we could realize your dream. But—I'm afraid such an expedition is impossible. If you knew more about Oberon, you'd realize it."

"That's right," muttered Whitey Jones, his excitement ebbing. "The terrific volcanic heat and awful lava flows of that moon have killed everyone who tried to explore it. Even the big expeditions the Company sent to survey it never returned."

"But my father left directions how to combat the dangers there," reminded Aline. "His direction to make a landing only at one spot—he must have meant that, by doing so, it would be possible to land safely on Oberon."

"That's rather a slim assurance to go on," North said thoughtfully. "I can't believe any landing place on Oberon would be safe. Yet he must have learned something, as you say. It might just be feasible to land there so—"

"Of course it is!" declared the ebullient Connor, his red face glistening excitedly. "Hell, here's a chance for us to get to space again. Are we going to turn it down?"

North shrugged. "There's more to it than that. We haven't any ship, and no money to buy one. That's why I say it's impossible."

"But I already have a ship," Aline said natter-of-factly. "I used the money I received from selling the bit of levium to buy an old twelve-man cruiser from the Company. I'm receiving the title to it this afternoon."

She added more doubtfully, "It's a pretty old ship, I'm afraid. It was in the Company's Saturn run until they condemned it. But it was the only craft I could find at that price that would be able to go as far as Uranus."

"If it's got two plates that'll hold together, we'll nurse it out to Uranus and back," boasted Connor. "We're none of your new style 'scientific' spacemen—not we, that sailed in the crazy old first rocket ships."

John North felt the enthusiasm of the others kindling him. He glimpsed a heaven-sent opportunity to see space once more—and to win a rich prize that would mean direly needed help for his old, broken, forgotten comrades.

"Whitey and I will go with you and look over the ship," he told Aline eagerly. "But what about equipment? What about the double outfit of anti-heaters your father mentioned?"

"We could get that stuff better out at Uranus itself, at Moontown on Titania," pointed out Whitey. "They use them a lot out there."

Aline's face fell. "But that will take money. And I'm afraid I haven't enough left."

"Never you mind, we'll worry about that when we get out there," Connor blithely reassured her. "We'll get that stuff if we have to steal it. Ah, it's going to be like old times again, roaring out the old space trail with the cycs singing a tune to us all the way."

"We go day after tomorrow, don't we, John?" Steenie asked North with his bright smile. "You said we go back to space day after tomorrow."

"Sure we do, Steenie," North said gently. "Day after tomorrow."

"I'll get my kit ready," Steenie said eagerly, shuffling away to a corner. "I'll be all ready."

"Poor, space-struck feller," muttered old Peters. "He thinks we're goin' to take him with us."

Whitey stared at the old man. "You don't think you're going?"

"I'd like to know why not?" flared Peters. His faded eyes snapped. "I was in rockets when you were wet-nosed infants, and don't you ever forget it! I'd like to *see* you leave me behind—"

North and Whitey went down the stairs with Aline Laurel. "The woman who runs this place will take care of Peters and Steenie while we're gone," he told her. "But we'll have to be diplomatic with them."

"They—they make me want to cry," she said in a low voice.

TWILIGHT was descending on the huddled, raucous life of Killiston Street as the two men and the girl made their way toward the spaceport. The dusk was deeper by the time they reached the shipyard where the Company kept its surplus stores and equipment and condemned ships.

It was surrounded by a high fence, an extensive establishment of metal supply houses, looming storage tanks of fuel, oxygen and water, and orderly stacks of rocket-tubes, cyc-parts and hull plates. A brawny watchman at the gate who wore the Company gray recognized Aline and let them enter.

She led the way to a corner dock from which towered the tarnished torpedo-like metal bulk of a twelve-man long distance cruiser. It had dents of meteors in its hull plates. The projecting rocket-tubes looked worn and shaky. It bore the name *Meteor* on its bows.

They went inside and Aline watched anxiously while Whitey and North inspected the equipment with practiced eyes. They started up the tarnished cyclotrons and listened closely to their throbbing drone, checking the controls by tramping hard on the cyc-pedal in front of the pilot chair. The old ship quivered violently in its dock to the vibration.

"Well, frankly, this craft has seen plenty of service and its Number Three and Number Five cycs aren't so hot," Whitey told Aline as they emerged from the ship. "But she ought to get us to Uranus all right."

North nodded agreement. "But we'll have to avoid running close to anything in space. Those controls are none too responsive."

Aline sighed in relief. "I'm glad the ship will do." Then she pointed across the yard. "There comes Mr. Carson, from whom I bought her."

Two men in the gray uniform of the Company were approaching. Carson was a stocky, middle-aged man, but his companion was a pleasant-faced, clean-cut younger fellow with the stars of an official on his collar. North and Whitey both stiffened with dislike at the sight of the Company uniforms.

"My friends like the *Meteor*, Mr. Carson," Aline said eagerly. "We'll be able to take off soon."

Carson shook his head. "Well, now, Miss Laurel, I'm afraid we'll have to call off our deal. It seems I can't sell you the *Meteor*, after all."

"But I gave you my check for it!" Aline cried in blank surprise.

Carson handed her a slip of paper. "Here it is back, Miss Laurel. Mr. Philip Sidney, this gentleman here, will explain it all to you."

Philip Sidney, the younger Company official, had an expression of discomfort on his clean-cut face as he stepped forward.

"It's orders from the Main Office, Miss Laurel," he told the girl. "The General Manager says we can't sell you any ship. But we'll be glad to provide a new craft and crew for your expedition, if you'll make arrangement to share with the Company any mineral levium you may find."

North asked the girl sharply, "Did you tell the Company why you wanted a ship, what you were going after?"

She shook her head bewilderedly. "No, I didn't. I can't understand—"

Philip Sidney shrugged. "We know you're going after levium, Miss Laurel. The Company has never credited the stories that a big deposit of it exists on Oberon, nor the rumors that your father once found it. But a few weeks ago, you sold a small quantity of levium to a certain firm. We learned of that at once, of course. It didn't take much figuring to deduce that your father *had* located the stuff, and that you were going after it now."

"And so your precious Company decided at once to cut in on it?" John North snapped. "Is that it?"

"Yes...that has to be it," declared Whitey Jones. "So that's the Company's idea of the proper 'arrangement' that Miss Laurel must make with you to get a ship, huh?"

Philip Sidney flushed. "It's the Main Office's orders, and I'm only obeying them in this. If Miss Laurel will concede the Company an eighty percent share of all precious minerals found, we'll provide her with a ship and crew."

"Eighty percent?" cried Aline Laurel unbelievingly. "Why, that's outrageous. I won't do it…"

Sidney shrugged a little uncomfortably. "Then I'm afraid you'll never get a ship. Only the Company has any to sell, you know."

WHITEY JONES, his massive face dark with rage, balled his fist and stepped forward. "Why, you dirty—"

"Hold it, Whitey," North interrupted. "This fellow is just taking orders, as he says. It'll do no good to take it out on him. You just can't buck the Company, and that's all there is to it."

North turned heavily to Aline.

"You'd better think over their proposition. It's robbery, of course—but you'd still make a fortune and otherwise you'll never get anything."

Though he kept his face and voice calm, North felt dead inside. His brief, wild hope of getting back to space, of helping his old comrades, of recapturing lost youth once more, had passed like a tantalizing dream.

"That's right, Miss Laurel," Philip Sidney was saying earnestly. "Twenty percent is a lot better than nothing. You ought to consider it."

"I'll never agree to such a thing." Aline Laurel retorted defiantly. "My father's friends are my partners, and I'm not going back on them…" She turned angrily away.

But she and North and Whitey were downheartedly silent as they walked slowly back to the drab lodging-house. Dusk had become night and the blue electro-lights were coming softly on along Killiston Avenue. Already there were crowds in the tawdry pleasure-houses that lay in wait to fleece the crews of docked spaceships. From the spaceport came the dull *blam-blam* of a landing ship.

North broke the heavy silence that had lain between them as they walked along the crowded, noisy street.

"We're grateful for your loyalty to us," he told the girl. "But there's no need of it. Sidney was giving you good advice."

Aline's eyes flashed. "He's despicable. Going back on the deal after they'd sold me the ship—"

"Oh, he's just obeying orders and didn't seem to like it any too well himself," North told her. "He's right—twenty percent beats nothing."

"Sure, there's no use losing a fortune for yourself just to help us guys," Whitey rumbled. His massive face fell a little as he added, "But it's going to be a little tough telling the others."

Connor and the others in the dusty garret sprang up eagerly as the three entered.

"Did you see the ship, Johnny?" asked the Irishman excitedly. "Will she make the span to Uranus all right?"

"How about the fuel?" Hansen asked earnestly. "How soon can we start?"

North felt a little heartsick as he told them what had happened, and saw the crushed, beaten look that came back onto their aging faces.

"Never you mind, Miss," Connor told Aline gallantly. "It was a fine thing you tried to do for us. But we can always take care of ourselves."

"I want you to listen to me," the girl told them emphatically. "In the first place, my name is Aline, and not *Miss*. In the second place, I'm not accepting any such offer as the Company is making."

"But you can't sacrifice your own interests to help us," North expostulated. "It would be foolish—"

"Not so foolish as it would be to go into partnership with the Company," she declared. "You know the high-handed way they do business, as well as I. Do you think that once they learned all I could tell them, gotten my father's notes, and then secured the levium, that they'd really give me a share of it?"

"She's probably right," said Connor softly, almost under his breath. "Those slick pirates who run the Company wouldn't hesitate for a moment at cheating her out of her share. It'd be one of the least of their misdeeds."

NORTH felt troubled. He knew that it was the truth. The Company's remorseless and unscrupulous methods were proverbial. Its Main Office was interested only in squeezing every imaginable profit from every transaction.

"It's true they'd be tricky to deal with," he told Aline slowly, frowning. "But what else can you do, unless you give it up completely?"

"I'm not going to give it up," she declared firmly. "We're going to Oberon after that levium, as we planned. And we're going in my ship. They sold me the *Meteor* and it's mine and I'm going to use it."

Whitey shook his massive head. "They'll never let you have it or any other ship. They'll hold the case up in space court for years if you sue them over it."

"We won't go to court," Aline retorted. "We'll simply take our ship, leave the check for them, and be on our way."

"But they'd charge you with space piracy and theft," North protested. "They'd—"

And then North stopped. He looked around at the others, and saw in every face the same excited, sudden determination that he too felt.

"They'd charge you with space piracy and theft," he repeated softly, "but we'd already be gone. *If* we could do it, *if* we could actually get away—"

Whitey's face was all it up. "Hell…why can't we? What do all these modern pettifogging space laws mean to us? The ship is rightfully Aline's, law or no law. And if we can use it to lift that levium and give our old comrades a new lease on life—I say let's take it…"

"Now you're talking!" crowed Connor, his red face glistening. "We'll charge in there, grab the craft, and be away before they know what's happened. Come on, let's do it now…"

"Not so fast, you wild monkey," growled Jan Dorak. His stolid face turned inquiringly to North. "What about fuel and equipment, Johnny?"

North planned breathlessly. "We'd have to pull this at night. It would be a matter of overpowering the watchmen and then fueling up the ship before the alarm gets out. All of that anti-heater equipment we'd have to pick up out at Uranus, on Titania moon—if we got there."

He added warningly, "But the Company will raise a storm all over the System to stop us. They've got stations almost everywhere, too."

"Ha, I'd like to see some of these young pretty boys they call spacemen stop us," grunted Hansen. His blue eyes had a frosty light.

It was as though a new breath of life had been pumped into the aging men around North. They were all adventurers again. And now, after many gray years of Earthbound monotony, they were hearing adventure's siren call again.

CHAPTER THREE
Spaceward Ho

"CAN we do it tonight?" stolid Jan Dorak asked calmly.

"There's fuel and supplies to be considered," North muttered. "We could get fuel, oxygen and water for the bunkers there in the Company yard, if we could keep the electrolarms quiet. But food—"

"I can buy what supplies you need and get them to the yard there tonight," Aline offered eagerly.

"Hell, let's go tonight then!" burst out big Whitey. "Why shouldn't we when there's only a couple of watchmen between us and the space trail to fortune. Just give us your orders, Johnny."

"My orders?" North echoed amazedly. "What the devil, I'm not captain of this party. I'm still the cub, the youngest man in the outfit."

"That's just why you've got to be first officer," Whitey rumbled decisively. "You're the quickest, youngest pilot in the lot. My one arm lets me out, Connor is a cyc-man, and Hansen a navigator and you know how bad Dorak's eyes are. You're our best bet, and you know it."

The others chorused agreement. North frowned. "All right, but I'm damned if I won't feel out of place giving orders to you fellows. And this captain business only goes for the time being."

He talked rapidly. "Dorak, you go with Aline and bring a truck of space rations to that Company yard at exactly eleven tonight. Hansen, start plotting our preliminary course in a...C-curve toward Uranus. Connor, slip down to that yard and keep an eye on things inside. Whitey and I will be there at ten sharp."

As the others departed hastily, old Peters wheeled forward and asked an anxious question.

"You ain't forgettin' me and Steenie, Johnny? You wouldn't really leave us here, would you?"

"We've got to," North told him earnestly. "You know yourself that you're too old for a space jaunt, Peters. The shock of take-off would kill you."

The old man took it better than North had expected. "Well, maybe you're right," he mumbled. "Though I did want to see space again once more before I died."

"Aren't we going to sail with you, Johnny?" asked Steenie, a bewildered look in his vacant eyes. "Aren't you going to take us?"

"We can't, Steenie," North said gently. "Someone has to stay and look after Peters, don't you see? We want you to do that."

"But you'll need me. I'm a good pilot," Steenie said seriously. "They said I was the best pilot that ever took a spaceship out, didn't they, Whitey?"

Whitey, his massive face moved, nodded pityingly. "Yes, they said that, Steenie, and it was true. You were the greatest pilot of them all, back in those times."

"Sure, and we'll want you the next voyage," North told the space-struck man. "But this time I want you to stay. It's an order, Steenie."

Out of a dim, half-forgotten past, Steenie brought a sharp gesture of salute. "Yes, sir. I'll obey orders."

He and the old man in the wheelchair watched for the next few hours as North and Whitey feverishly helped Hansen plot the course they would have to follow to take the most feasible path toward Uranus, and pack their few spare space-jackets in compact kits.

Connor came hastening back into the room, his frog face crimson now with excitement.

"Just two watchmen down at that Company yard," he reported. "One at the front gate and one at the side."

"We can handle them," North declared. He glanced at his watch. "Time to go."

They looked uncertainly across the dim lit garret at old Peters, slumped in his chair with Steenie standing beside him.

"Ah, don't stop to blather goodbyes," grunted the old veteran. "You're just wasting time."

SILENTLY, North and the other three trooped down the dark stairs to the street. Shouldering their kits, they moved quietly along the bright, tawdry, noisy thoroughfare—toward the spaceport whose red and green tower-lights hung against the starry sky.

Rocket-flame curved skyward with a thunderous roar as a freighter climbed from its dock. North felt a thrill. It had been almost two years since he'd been to space. He felt tonight as though he was seventeen again, swaggering proudly with a younger Whitey toward Carew's crazy little ship that was to take them into the unknown.

They went more slowly as they approached the front gate of the Company's space-stores yard. North stopped in the shadow of a tower.

"We've got to get that gate open," North muttered. "Wait here."

He strode forward into the pool of light outside the gate, and urgently pushed the stud that rang a bell in the watchman's hut.

The watchman, a short, thickset man in the Company gray, came out and scrutinized him keenly through the bars of the gate.

"Mr. Sidney sent me over to get a report he left here today," North said nonchalantly. "Open up there, will you."

The watchman hesitated. "You're not in uniform," he remarked.

"I'm not one of your Company slaves," North retorted cheerfully. "I'm Sidney's buddy. Hurry up, man—I don't have all night."

A little doubtfully, the man unlocked the gate. "Let's see now, where's the ship *Meteor?*" North asked. "He left it in there, he said."

The watchman turned to point. "It's over—"

Thunk! The man went down like a bundle of rags as North's fist caught the angle of his jaw. North whistled a low note. Connor and Whitey and Hansen came in like swift shadows.

They bound and gagged the watchman efficiently, and then crept silently toward the side gate. The second watchman was soon tied up, too.

"Watch by the main gate, Whitey," North ordered. "Hansen…here's the watchman's electrolarm key. I imagine the things have to be punched on the hour. Go around and try to find everyone of them."

Then he gestured Connor. "Now for the fuel and oxygen. Come on…"

He and Connor raced toward the *Meteor.* The Irish cyc-man was chuckling under his breath as they ran between the looming supply houses.

"Ah, it's like the old days come to life again, Johnny! I remember a night when—"

North had reached the *Meteor* and was using the watchman's torch to search for the fuel, oxygen and water lines. They must be somewhere near the dock, he knew—and at last he found the three heavy metal pipelines that stemmed from towering tanks across the dark yard.

He and Connor scrambled around until they made fast the flexible pipe connections to the inlets in the side of the ship's hull.

"Go over to that fuel house and start the stuff pumping," North panted to his companion. "I'll watch the gauges and give you a two-flash signal when the bunkers are full."

Connor raced away. North soon heard a low throbbing of pumps over in the fuel house. And a few seconds later there was a whispering rustling from inside the pipes they had connected to the *Meteor's* inlets.

Powdered copper was being pumped through one of those pipes into the big fuel bunkers of the ship, to serve to feed the cyclotrons. Oxygen for the 'genator tanks was being forced under compression through a second pipe, and drinking water through a third.

North alertly watched the gauges inside the cramped control room, hunching in the pilot chair and using the torch for light. Hansen's head protruded suddenly into the crowded, shadowy little room.

"I think I got all the electrolarms," he reported tensely. "I was all over every corner of the yard."

"Okay, slide back out to the main gate to Whitey," North rapped to him. "I think Aline and Dorak just arrived with the rations."

THE gauges finally showed that the bunkers of the *Meteor* were full. North hastily flashed a signal, and the throbbing of pumps stopped. North was disconnecting the feed-lines when Connor came hurrying up.

Behind the Irishman materialized a small power truck, running without lights. Aline and Dorak hastily climbed down from its cab, while Whitey and Hansen appeared closely behind it.

Aline's face was a white blur in the darkness but her voice was thrilled as she reported to North. "I left my check for the ship on the watchman—and we have the rations here."

"Come on—let's get them in," sweated North. "Connor, get back to those cycs and start the injectors. We'll want to take off fast."

They were hauling the flat cases of concentrated foods into the dark ship, blundering and stumbling over each other in the narrow passageways inside, when there came a sharp warning whisper from Aline:

"I think somebody's coming…"

North jumped out into the darkness.

He heard a sound of faintly creaking wheels and then a shrill voice cut through the night.

"Are we 'bout ready to go, Johnny?"

"Damn…it's old Peters!" gasped Whitey. "How the devil did he get here?"

That mystery was soon explained. Steenie wheeled the old cripple's chair forward toward the ship.

"Thought you was goin' to leave the old man behind, eh?" cackled Peters. "Not much. Soon's you were gone, I told Steenie to wheel me here."

"Am I going in that ship, Johnny?" Steenie asked eagerly.

North groaned. "You've got to go back, Peters. You and Steenie can't come—"

"I'll come or know the reason why!" shrilled the old man's quivering voice. "You ain't goin' to cheat me out of my last chance to go to space. I'll come, or else I'll yell my head off right now."

"We'll have to let them come, Johnny," groaned Whitey. "If we don't, the old rascal will rouse the whole spaceport."

"All right, get them into the ship," North said helplessly. "Come on—we've got to get the rest of these rations aboard—"

Bong...bong...!

They jumped as somewhere in the darkness a bell began a clamorous, frantic clanging.

"I must have missed one of the electrolarms!" cried Hansen. "That jams everything—"

Distant cries of alarm could be heard over the hellish clangor of the electrolarm bell. Whistles shrilled, and big searchlights on the spaceport towers blazed out blue-white beams that swept rapidly toward this shipyard.

"Into the ship. We've got to let the rest of the rations go," North commanded. "There'll be Company police here in two minutes!"

Already sirens were whining in a rising crescendo. There was a distant roar of speeding rocket-cars dashing toward the shipyard.

Blue beams of the sweeping searchlight caught and held in a dazzling glare the spacemen as they tumbled into the ship.

"Connor, start the cycs!" blared North's voice. "Hansen, the door. Everyone in their space chairs..."

He leaped forward into the little control room and snapped the panel switch. Light leaped out from hooded lamps and gleamed off the bank of dials and throttles, and the space-stick and pedals.

North's hands buckled himself into the pilot chair with frantic speed, while big Whitey scrambled into the copilot seat beside him. The slam of the hermetic door was followed by a bursting, throbbing roar that shook the old ship in every strut. Connor had the cycs going.

NORTH'S hands closed tightly on the space-stick, centering it precisely for a keel-tube take-off.

"Blasting off!" he yelled back through the ship.

Through the window, he glimpsed a half-dozen rocket-cars rushing across the shipyard toward them. Men jumped from the cars, leveling heavy atom guns and shouting inaudible commands.

North was suddenly icy calm. The discipline of twenty years experience took possession of his body. Holding the space-stick precisely centered, his foot jammed the cyc-pedal to the floor.

Recoil springs screamed torturedly under his chair as the acceleration from point zero slammed down on him. Giant iron hands seemed to constrict his chest, preventing him from breathing, strangling him. His head roared and a red blur dimmed his vision.

But he glimpsed lights and docks and shouting men outside vanish as though by magic, as the raving energy of the cycs poured in a scorching blast from the keel tubes. The starred heavens overheard were rocking dizzily to the wild lurching of the upshooting *Meteor*.

North jerked the space-stick back a little, keeping the cyc-pedal floor-boarded. The atomic energy of the cycs, now partly diverted to the tail tubes, sent the old cruiser upward in a steep, swinging climb.

"Thought her thrust-struts were going to give!" he heard Whitey shouting thinly over the roar of cycs and tubes. "But they didn't—"

North made no answer, bending the space-stick farther and farther back. And the old *Meteor,* creaking, rocking and shuddering in every beam, climbed higher on a roaring slant into the star-decked heavens.

The spaceport lights were a red-green quadrangle of tiny size on the black globe below. They were roaring up out of the shadow of Earth's curve into the brassy glare of the Sun, and the air-friction alarms were shrieking wildly as the hull overheated.

North's laugh pealed out over the throbbing roar. "Clean blastoff. We slipped them nicely, Whitey."

His soul was throbbing in tune with the cycs in wild intoxication. The feel of the space-stick in his hands was like wine to him, and the brilliant stars of space were like luring beacons, and the old *Meteor* a magic ship capable of driving to the farthest reaches of infinity.

Old ship and old spacemen—both of them condemned and forgotten—going to space again... And now John North knew that he had not been really living in those dull, gray Earthbound months. He had only been sleeping, existing, waiting for this time when he could live again.

The flame of emotion on Whitey's massive face told him that his old comrade felt the same. They were out of the atmosphere now, and the friction alarms had fallen silent, and Earth was a convex green globe dropping away behind and below them.

Reluctantly, North eased his pressure on the cyc-pedal. The bursting roar of the cycs dropped to a steady drone. Its tail tubes roaring, the old ship throbbed out toward the far green spark that was distant Uranus.

ALINE LAUREL came into the control room, looking pale and shaken. North suddenly realized that it must be her first space voyage.

"You're sick?" he cried anxiously. "I might have known it—that start—I had to make it fast."

She shook her dark head. "No, I'm all right. But old Peters—he's hurt, John. The shock—"

Hastily, North called for Dorak to come forward and take the space-stick. He and Whitey hurried back along the shuddering catwalk to the bunkroom in which the old man was lying, the others bending over him.

One glance constricted North's heart. Peter's eyes were closed, his face blue, and a thin trickle of red was at the corner of his mouth.

"Unconscious, now," he murmured after examining the old man. "Internal injuries. I told him he couldn't stand the shock of take-off."

Aline's pale face held a question. "Will he—"

"He can't live," North said heavily. "It's only a matter of hours."

The others were silent. But Steenie looked at him with a faint distress in his clear, vacant eyes.

"Is Peters sick, Johnny?" he asked puzzledly.

The hours went by, but the old veteran's condition did not change. They were now flying out well toward the orbit of Mars, and North set the watches and extended the flight-curve Hansen had computed.

"We'll swing wide of Jupiter—to avoid the main space lanes," he told the others. "The Company will have police cruisers on the lookout for us, be sure of that. But they can't comb all space."

Whitey nodded soberly. "We can get to Uranus all right, if this craft keeps ticking. But if we have trouble off the space lanes—"

He didn't need to finish. The men all knew that a slow death by starvation or air-exhaustion would be their fate in such a case.

North looked intently at Uranus before he left the space-stick to Hansen. The green spark was brighter and bigger, now. Its moons were not yet visible to the unaided eye.

He felt a sense of unreality about this strange quest. A quest to the dreaded Thunder Moon for the levium that half the System thought so fabulous. Quest amid strange perils with only a dead man's word to guide them—

"John…Peters is coming to," Aline called him.

North hastened back to the bunkroom, with the others. The old veteran had opened his eyes. The faded blue eyes were dazed, bewildered, as they looked up at the anxious faces.

Then as old Peters looked beyond them, at the window with its vista of star-jeweled space, a queer expression of triumph, of happiness, lit his eyes. Almost contentedly, he closed them again.

"He's sleeping now," Aline said hopefully. "Maybe—"

North drew her gently away. He told Connor heavily, "You wrap him up, Mike. We'll give him a space burial."

In dead silence, the men moved toward their old companion as North led the girl to the main cabin. She looked up at him incredulously.

"He can't be dead!" she exclaimed.

"I've seen lots of men die in space, and they all go like that," North told her. "But old Peters went happy—he knew, before he died, that he was back in space again."

THEY brought the wrapped body out and gently placed it inside the airlock of the main door. Steenie stood, watching with his vacant blue eyes wide and puzzled. The others turned to North.

"Can you remember the space burial ritual?" asked Whitey.

North shook his head. "Nothing but the opening words, *'Since this man our comrade—'* How about you, Whitey?"

Whitey shook his massive head somberly. "It's been so long since I heard it used, that I've forgotten it long ago."

North looked around at the other two, but both Connor and Dorak shook their heads.

"Don't seem quite right to bury old Peters without saying the words, but I guess we'll have to," said Dorak sadly.

Then Steenie surprised them all. The space-struck sailor had been staring intently at the wrapped body in the airlock. As though it had brought something to his dimmed mind, he stepped forward and began to speak simply.

"Since this man our comrade has reached life's end in perilous traverse between world and world, and may not lie in any world to await the judgment of eternity—"

They were all rigidly silent, startled, wonder stricken, as Steenie's quiet voice rolled on, speaking the words that long ago Mark Carew had spoken for Gorham Johnson, his great chieftain—those classic words that had been used ever since for the ritual of space burial.

"—and therefore we commit this body to the great deeps of the infinite, to wander the vastnesses of the void until such day as the last summons shall call from space its dead."

Steenie's voice stopped. North and the others looked at him breathlessly, half-expecting that a miracle had restored his dimmed reason. But Steenie's face was as blank, his blue eyes as vacant, as ever.

"I remembered it all, didn't I?" he said proudly.

"Yes, Steenie," North said unsteadily. "You remembered it all."

He made a signal with his hand. Hansen, at the space-stick, gave the *Meteor* a sharp snap-turn with a blast of the lateral tubes.

The wrapped corpse of the old veteran was thrown clear from the airlock, and drifted rapidly off into space. They all watched silently, until the dot was no longer visible against the stars.

"There goes the last of Gorham Johnson's crew," muttered Whitey.

"You know," said Jan Dorak thoughtfully, "it wasn't so far from here that Johnson himself was given space burial. It'd be queer if old Peters would find his chief out there, wouldn't it?"

Aline had turned away. North followed her back to the stern cabin and found her there, face pressed against a window, sobbing.

"It was my fault it happened...all my fault," she choked out when North turned her tear-stained face around. "If I hadn't proposed this quest out to Thunder" Moon, he wouldn't have been killed—"

"Why, Aline, Peters died happy," North told her. "It's what he wanted above everything else—to die in space, to be buried in space."

He soothed her. And she clung to him, burying her head on his shoulder.

But all North's wild exhilaration was gone. And as he looked out of the window at Uranus' largening green spark, he could not help feeling that it was into an ever-deepening shadow that they were flying on their desperate quest to Thunder Moon.

CHAPTER FOUR
In Moontown

JOHN NORTH had not been to Uranus for four years. It was with sharp emotion that he watched its great green sphere expand across the sky.

He spoke to the one-armed giant in the copilot chair beside him. "Do you remember, Whitey—coming in toward it with Carew for the first landing?"

Whitey Jones nodded with deep feeling. "And how excited we youngsters all were, eh? It doesn't seem twenty years ago."

North's mind forced away those old memories, to consider their present difficulties. Every day of the long, curving flight out through the System had increased his foreboding.

They were, strictly speaking, pirates. And though Earth law did not yet reach to this wild frontier of space, the power of the Company did. There was a Company station at Moontown. And to Moontown they must go, somehow to procure there the anti-heat equipment vital to their quest.

North raised his voice. "Aline...Mike...we'll have to start the brake-blasts soon. Better get ready to strap in."

The others came forward to the control room. Connor's red face was carefree as ever. The long, monotonous days that had made Dorak more silent and Hansen more brooding had not affected the reckless Irishman.

But Aline Laurel was pale from the weeks of ship-air, her dark eyes very large in her white, fine face as she peered eagerly ahead.

"Uranus looks so huge from this close," she breathed. "And so frightening."

"It's plenty big and plenty bad," North admitted, eyeing the great planet. "It's the stormiest of all the major worlds."

Uranus was a forbidding spectacle. Its mighty green sphere blotted out half the heavens, so close now was the *Meteor.* Yet little could be seen of its surface, wrapped as it was in cloudy atmosphere hundreds of miles deep. That cloudy blanket was boiling with black storms, which moved across the surface at hurricane speed.

Three of the great planet's moons were visible to them, from the sunward side. The two little satellites Ariel and Umbriel were close to the planet, creeping across its face. Farther out, and nearer to their approaching ship, marched the larger moon Titania. The dense, wild jungle with which it was covered lent it a deeper shade of green than the parent planet.

"It looks almost as wild as Uranus," murmured Aline doubtfully, gazing at this moon that was their immediate destination.

"It's not as bad, though the jungles are full of queer beasts and those outlandish Titanian aborigines," rumbled Whitey. He pointed to a dark spot on the green satellite. "That's Moontown, the rawest, wildest boomtown in the System."

"That's where we're going to try to get the anti-heat equipment?" asked the girl earnestly. "Are you sure we'll be able to get it there?"

North said grimly, "I'm sure they'll *have* it there, if that's what you mean. They use anti-heat equipment a lot for prospecting in the southern volcanic region of Uranus. But as to how we're going to get it, without money or credit—"

"Ah, quit worrying and leave that to me," Connor retorted confidently. "Didn't I tell you I'd get the stuff? I've got friends here."

They were turning to go back to the main cabin and strap in, when Whitey pointed his single arm and said in a quick, low voice:

"There's Oberon now, coming out of eclipse…"

THE fourth satellite of Uranus was coming out from behind the bulk of the planet. Aline cried out at sight of it.

The moon was a terrifying sight. It was a sullen crimson sphere, wrapped in a shallow atmosphere heavily laden with dark smoke. Through rifts in that gloomy, smoky haze could be glimpsed flaming volcanic continents—lands of fire upon whose burning coasts surged the evil crimson tide of a great ocean of molten lava.

Thunder Moon, lurid hell-world of the System, a playground of unchained volcanic forces that made it resemble some inferno of ancient superstition. Its red rays struck through the window of the flying ship, mingling with the softer planet-light to paint the tense faces of the staring group.

"Surely no amount of anti-heat equipment will make it safe to land *there,*" gasped Aline Laurel.

"It wouldn't, ordinarily," John North admitted. "But your father's directions indicate that he found a spot where it was just possible to land by using heavy anti-heat equipment. We'll have to gamble on that."

He added guardedly, "Go back and strap in now. I've got to start cutting in toward Titania."

The *Meteor* came down toward Titania in a long, swinging sweep, North expertly using the lateral tubes to edge them into a closing spiral and the brake-blasts to slow their speed. Even so, by the time the old ship roared down through the atmosphere of the moon in a descending slant across the green jungle, Moontown was being overtaken by approaching night.

The town lay in the dusk as a huddle of flimsy chromalloy shacks, situated at the center of a raw clearing blasted out of the jungle. A little north of it was a smaller clearing that held the spaceport. North brought the creaking old ship down toward the red and green beacons with practiced smoothness. He kept it hovering a moment, riding the flaming jets of its keel tubes, and then let it sink to the ground.

"Good landing, Johnny," mumbled Whitey as they unstrapped. "You haven't lost the touch."

The others were getting out of their chairs, back in the main cabin. Hansen unscrewed the door, and a flood of warm, damp air heavy with pungent scents of decaying vegetation rushed in.

"Moon-shoes on, everybody," North warned, stooping to buckle on the auxiliary lead soles himself.

They stepped out into the gathering dusk, stepping onto churned-up soil still smoking from the rocket blasts. Shapes of other ships, freighters and a couple of cruisers, loomed vaguely across the spaceport.

Queer creatures like travesties of men came running eagerly toward them. Aline Laurel shrank back with a little cry. These were green, manlike creatures, with enormous pupil-less eyes in their parrot-beaked faces. They wore rags of cast-off Earth clothing, and extended fingerless hands.

"Sal, Urmen!" they screeched to North. "Sal!"

"They're just Titanian aborigines," North reassured the scared girl. "They're begging for salt—give the poor devils a little, Hansen."

Whitey gripped his arm, nodding his massive head toward one of the two gleaming cruisers on the other side of the spaceport.

"That's a fast Company cruiser, Johnny, and it just got in before we did. See, the ground's still hot from its landing jets."

NORTH stiffened with alarm. "We might have expected it," he muttered. "The Company could send a cruiser out here from Earth and it'd get here before we did, by following the regular space-lanes."

"If they try to take the *Meteor* away from us, it'll be fight," flared Whitey. "Earth law doesn't run past Jupiter. We hold our ship…"

The others muttered agreement. The hatred of these men for the Company that had so long barred them from employment flamed out quickly.

"Take it easy—it hasn't come to a fight yet," rapped North. "Maybe the Company's planning to let us go on to Thunder Moon, so they can follow us right to the levium there. Or they may figure that we'll have to come to them to get anti-heat equipment here."

"The company's not the only source in Moontown for anti-heaters," declared Hansen. "You can get them at the supply houses that outfit prospectors for Uranus."

"You can, if you have money or credit," muttered Jan Dorak.

"I can get the credit, boys," announced Mike Connor buoyantly. "I know a chap here who'll stake us for the equipment, for a share of the profits. It's Charles Berdeau, who runs a pleasure-house here."

"Berdeau?" rumbled Whitey. "I never heard anything good about *that* interplanetary rascal. They ran him out of Jupiter."

John North shrugged. "We'll have to get help where we can. Mike and I will go into the town and look up this Berdeau fellow. You and the others had better stay here, Whitey—in case the Company officers here do try to take the *Meteor.*"

"Can I go with you?" Aline Laurel asked North eagerly.

"I'd rather you stayed," he told her earnestly. "Moontown is a tough, wild place—no place for a girl. And there may be trouble there."

He sensed her disappointment as he and Connor buckled on atom-pistols and strode away through the deepening dusk.

It was almost completely dark by the time they crossed the spaceport and started along the short road through the jungle to the town. The damp air was heavy with rank scent of the dense forest of fern-like trees. Queer "floating flowers" drifted against their faces, leaving lingering traces of exquisite perfume. Far off in the jungle a tree-cat wailed blood-chillingly, while overhead in the darkness was the leathery rattle of a passing dragon-hawk's wings. Moon-bats called screechingly.

The stars blazed brightly down upon them. But over at the east horizon there was a ghostly uprush of green light from behind the horizon. It waxed stronger by the minute.

Then the colossal green shield of Uranus pushed up into the sky, filling half the heavens as it poured down viridescent brilliance like an incredibly huge emerald moon.

Conner uttered an ebullient exclamation as they approached the lights of Moontown.

"Ah…this is living again, Johnny. And I was afraid we'd rust our lives out in that dusty garret on Earth."

North felt it too, that hot tingling of long-dead youth coming back again. It was good to be out amongst the far, wild worlds once again.

But he curbed his excitement, reminding himself of the desperate urgency of their mission here. "This Berdeau—where will we find him?"

"He'll be somewhere around, if they haven't hanged him yet," Connor said blithely. Then as they came to the edge of the town, the Irishman uttered an exclamation. "Look at that street…"

Moontown was blazing with life tonight, under the green glow of mighty Uranus. The heart of the boom city was a single short street, lined solidly with gambling halls, drinking joints and similarly dubious establishments. Behind this street, the warehouses and outfitting shops of the Company and independent traders were dark, but along this street there was a brilliant glow of "ion-signs" beckoning to pleasure.

DRUNKEN Earthmen reeled through the crowd in the muddy street, prospectors squandering in a short spree the radium or platinum they had risked their lives for on Uranus. Little groups of the parrot-beaked green Titanians pestered with their begging cry of "Sal, Urmen!" or peered wonderingly into the brilliant buildings whence came the throb and blare of brassy music.

North had seen planetary boomtowns before, and they were always much the same. Always they were haunted by a riff-raff of crooked gamblers and outlaws and star-girls, and cunning traders and promoters who garnered the wealth that hardy adventurers wrested from alien perils. But never, even on Jupiter in the old wild days, had he seen such a roaring tempo as ruled here beneath the green glow of great Uranus.

"A fellow could have a fight or a frolic here, Johnny!" Mike Connor exclaimed, his frog face grinning.

"We're not here for fun," North rapped. "What about this Berdeau chap?"

"Talk of the devil and you see his sign," Connor replied, pointing. "See that, Johnny?"

The ion sign he pointed at was glowing from a false-fronted chromalloy hall further down the street—*Berdeau's Pleasure Palace!*

They paused when they reached its wide-open doors. The big, krypton-lighted room inside was a crowded bedlam—clatter of glasses along the bar, roaring voices of intoxicated men, brassy blare of a music-machine spouting a dance tune, all adding to the uproar.

Burly prospectors who still had the greenish pallor of weeks on Uranus upon their faces were clustered thickest around the bar and the gambling machines in back. Mingling with them, coaxing them to squander their money more quickly, were hard-eyed "star-girls," as the System nicknamed the Earthgirl clip joint hostesses who followed the boom towns from world to world.

North and Connor pushed to the bar, and the Irishman asked a question of the sweating, overworked bartender. Then he turned to North.

"Berdeau's somewhere in back. You wait here, Johnny, and I'll find him."

North ordered Martian wine and drank the thin, sweet stuff slowly, absently listening to the roaring boasts of the drunken Earthman by him.

"—an' that's how I made my strike on South Uranus, partner. I tell you, I can *smell* platinum. I got me a fortune to take back home—"

North smiled bitterly to himself. The drunken prospector, he thought, had about one chance in a million of ever getting his fortune back to Earth. The swindlers and crooks of Moontown would see to that.

Through the uproar of the place there cut a sharp feminine voice. "Let go of my wrist, you big lug!"

North turned. One of the star-girls in the throng, a small blonde girl in a scanty white synthesilk dress, was furiously trying to free herself from a flushed-faced, angry, rough Earthman radium miner.

"No you don't, sister!" the red-faced miner was bellowing. "You got me to spend all my money—now you're not going to walk out on me."

North turned cynically back to his drink. The sordid incident did not interest him. But in a moment he turned sharply around again.

He had heard Mike Connor's voice loudly raised. "Quit badgering the lady, you big ape!" Connor was telling the angry radium miner. "Can't you see she's had enough of you?"

"Who are you to give me orders?" bellowed the man to Connor.

North groaned. "That damned fool Irishman. Fighting over a star-girl—"

CONNOR had belligerently interposed himself between the star-girl and the infuriated, half-intoxicated miner. North started forward to drag the too-chivalrous Irishman away.

Then someone yelled warning. The furious miner had suddenly drawn the heavy atom-pistol at his belt and was leveling it at Connor and the girl. His rough face was livid with rage.

"I'll blast you both down!" he shouted hoarsely at Connor. "You're in with that crooked little—"

North could have flashed his own atom-gun but he didn't. Without hesitation, he dived for the raging miner's legs in a flying tackle that bowled the man off his feet.

The fellow's atom-pistol let go in a scorching blast past North's ear, as they grappled on the floor. Then North glimpsed an opening and smashed hard with his fist. It cracked upon the miner's jutting jaw and the man went limp.

North kicked the fallen atom-pistol away and rose to his feet, breathing hard.

"Haul that space tramp out of here!" shouted the bartender, and a waiter hurried to drag the senseless miner outside.

The uproar in Berdeau's Pleasure Palace, which had quieted for the few moments of the incident, resumed. A fight was nothing new here.

North had jerked Connor angrily off the central floor. "You big idiot," he said scathingly to the Irishman. "Starting a row in here…when we're in trouble enough as it is."

"But I couldn't let that drunken bum push a lady around, Johnny," defended Connor.

"A lady? That star-girl?" repeated North witheringly. "Don't be ridiculous."

Someone touched his arm. North turned, and then his face darkened. It was the star-girl over whom the fight had started.

She was an almost childishly small figure, in her scanty, brazenly revealing white synthesilk dress. Her blonde head came barely to North's shoulder. But there was nothing childish about her face, the pert prettiness of which was hardened by too much makeup and too-wise blue eyes.

"I'm Nova Smith," she told North. "And thanks a lot for jumping that crazy drunk."

"You needn't thank me—I don't go around fighting over star-girls," North retorted with dislike. "I was merely trying to save this fool Irishman from getting blasted."

The star-girl bristled. "Nice and friendly, aren't you? Did I ask either of you to mix in? I can take care of myself."

"Your kind of woman usually can," North answered contemptuously.

"Now, Johnny, that's no way to be talking to a pretty girl," Connor reproved gallantly. His frog face wrinkled at the girl in what he believed to be a winning smile. "He's just upset, Miss Nova—"

"You'll be upset by the toe of my foot if you don't get going and find this fellow Berdeau," John North warned him ominously. "And don't tell him too much—*I'll* present the deal to him."

Connor hastened away through the noisy crowd. North turned moodily back to his half-finished goblet of Martian wine at the bar.

The star-girl followed him and stood appraising him with coolly insolent blue eyes. "Old-time space-sailor, aren't you?" she said. "Sure, I can tell you fellows a mile away."

"Look, I'm not buying you any drinks if that's what you're hanging around for," North told her brutally. "Clip someone else."

Nova Smith shrugged her bare shoulders. "All right, sailor. But here's a tip, in exchange for what you did. Watch yourself, if you're going into any deal with Berdeau. He's as crooked as they come."

"He's your boss, isn't he?" North said skeptically.

"No one is my boss, sailor," flared the star-girl. "I work here in Berdeau's place drumming up trade, but he doesn't own me and nobody else does. So don't you talk as though—"

She stopped. John North wasn't listening. He had suddenly stiffened as he saw three men enter the noisy room and look around.

They were all in the Company's gray uniform, and all were armed. Their leader was Philip Sidney, the young Company officer with whom North and his friends had clashed on Earth.

Sidney's gaze fixed on North. At once, his pleasant young face became grim. He and his two companions started purposefully toward North.

CHAPTER FIVE
The Attack

NORTH'S hand dropped toward the atom-pistol at his belt. He felt taut inside, for he knew that a crisis was at hand.

He knew now that Philip Sidney had been sent here in that Company cruiser that had beaten them to Uranus. That showed the deep determination of the Company to possess the levium that he and his comrades were seeking.

"Trouble is coming," North rapped to the star-girl, without turning. "There may be a fight. Better get out of here."

Nova Smith glanced quickly from his face to the three approaching Company men. "So you're in trouble with the Company, sailor? What's the angle?"

North had no time to answer. Sidney stood confronting him. The two Company men behind him had their hands near their atom-pistols.

"I thought you'd be in one of these places," Sidney said accusingly to North. "We heard you just got in. And I'm demanding that you turn over the *Meteor* to its rightful owners, the Company."

"Aline Laurel is rightful owner of that ship," North retorted coolly. "She bought it and paid for it."

"That forced sale was illegal and you know it," said Sidney.

North shrugged. "Earth law doesn't run out here on the frontier. What are you going to do about it?"

He was ready for an explosion. But Philip Sidney made no move toward his weapon. The young Company officer's voice dropped earnestly.

"North, I have to obey my orders whether I like them or not. But I'll tell you this, man to man—you ought to be shot if you take a fine girl like Miss Laurel out there into the dangers of Thunder Moon."

Sidney's clean-cut young face was flushed with anxiety. His sincerity was so apparent that North could not help feeling a certain liking for him. He had to remind himself harshly that he was talking to an officer of the hated Company.

"You're mighty worried about Miss Laurel," North jeered. "So worried that you'll be trailing right after us to Oberon, won't you?"

Philip Sidney shrugged helplessly. "I see you won't listen to reason, North. I'm sorry."

He turned away, the other two Company men following him out of Berdeau's establishment. North looked after them with narrowed eyes.

What orders had the Company given Sidney? He felt sure that they would be orders to follow North's expedition to Oberon and the levium, rather than to seize the ship. Anyway, they couldn't seize the *Meteor* with Whitey and the others on guard against just such an attempt.

"So you're going to Thunder Moon, sailor?" Nova Smith was saying. She shook her blonde head. "That's a messy way to kill yourself."

North looked at the star-girl with ironic amusement. "You're going to tell me how dangerous it is? I was out here when none of this riff-raff had ever heard of Uranus, and when you were in your cradle back on Earth."

Connor pushed through the crowd, his red face perspiring as he led another man up to North.

"This…John…is Charlie Berdeau," Connor introduced buoyantly. "Knew him back on Jupiter, when he was running a Jovopolis gambling joint. Used to clean me out there after every voyage, didn't you, Charlie?"

BERDEAU lit a green *rial* cigarette. Over the glow of the atomite lighter, his bold black eyes insolently appraised North's shabby figure.

The gambler was lean and dark, handsome in a faintly wolfish way. There was something too prominently predatory about the dashing good looks of his aquiline face, the gleam of his white teeth. His rich black synthesilk suit was of finest cut, and a beautiful Callistan fire opal smoldered on his slender white hand.

"Connor tells me you need a stake for a promising expedition," drawled Berdeau with apparent disinterest.

North nodded curtly. "We need double anti-heat equipment for a twelve man cruiser, and at least ten heavy insulite suits with individual anti-heaters."

"That's a big order of anti-heat equipment," Berdeau frowned. "Where are you going?"

"To Oberon," North answered levelly.

Berdeau burst into a laugh. "Don't tell me you're going there to hunt for levium?"

"What's so amusing about that?" North retorted.

Berdeau chuckled. "There's never a month passes but some old space-rat comes in here to tell me how he's going to hunt for the mythical levium on Thunder Moon. You're about the hundredth that's wanted a stake."

"Did the others show you anything like this?" North demanded flatly.

He held out the little lead-glass vial he had borrowed from Aline. The shining blue grain of levium in it, pressing uncannily against the top of the vial, instantly erased the amusement from Berdeau's face.

"Did that levium come from Thunder Moon?" he asked swiftly.

"It did, and there's a lot more of it there, and we know where it is and how to reach it," North told him.

Berdeau's black eyes glowed with interest. "That's different. Perhaps...perhaps we can talk business. Come into my office."

"Said the spider to the fly," flipped Nova Smith.

Berdeau turned angrily on the blonde star-girl. "You keep out of this—I've had enough trouble with you. Find Lenning and Kells and Darm and send them to me."

North and Connor followed the interplanetary gambler through the noisy, reveling crowd into a small office.

Berdeau's floridly handsome face was eager as he asked, "Now, just where is the levium on Oberon? How do you figure to land on that hellish moon without being destroyed?"

John North laughed curtly. "You don't really think I'd tell you that? Here's our proposition: Stake us to the anti-heat equipment, and we'll sign a contract giving you one tenth of the levium we find."

The gambler frowned. "You ask me to put up twenty thousand dollars worth of equipment, yet you don't trust me."

North shrugged. "The secret isn't mine, and I can't give it away."

"But you can at least tell me more about it," Berdeau persuaded.

NORTH briefly narrated the tale of how Aline Laurel's father had found the levium, and of his small legion of old-time spacemen they had formed to go after it, and of the Company's opposition.

Berdeau's eyes narrowed. "If the Company's after it, there must be something to it," the gambler muttered thoughtfully.

There was suppressed excitement in his face. He paced the little office for a moment and then appeared to come rapidly to a decision.

He thrust out his hand. "North, you may not trust me, but I'm going to trust you. I'm going to stake you to the equipment you need, and I won't ask you for any contract—your word is good enough for me."

Berdeau went to the door. "We'll buy the anti-heat equipment and take it to your ship right away, before the Company can interfere. Wait till I get the money."

"Now we're getting somewhere!" Connor exclaimed ebulliently as the gambler went out. "Didn't I tell you I'd fix things up, Johnny?"

But North felt a deep uneasiness. He hated doing business with one of the birds of prey who followed wealth from world to world. He didn't entirely trust the handsome gambler despite the man's apparent frankness.

Still, North told himself troubledly, there was no way they could lose by the deal. He hadn't given away the secret of the levium's location, and without that, no one could double-cross them.

He and Connor went out and found Berdeau talking earnestly to his three men. Lenning was a hulking, heavy-faced Earthman with an expressionless stare. Kells and Darm were hard-faced younger men.

"We're all ready," Berdeau told North effusively. "Lenning and the boys will help you load the stuff. We've got a rocket-truck."

As they started out through the crowd, Nova Smith caught at North's sleeve. The blonde star-girl's pert face was anxious.

"Sailor, I want to talk to you a moment," she said urgently.

"Sorry, but we're in a hurry," John North replied brusquely, brushing past her to follow the others out the door.

"You've made a conquest, Johnny," chuckled Connor.

"A star-girl," muttered North contemptuously.

"Ah, she's a good kid," defended the Irishman. "The trouble with you is that you've got Aline on your mind."

The rocket-truck rattled down the noisy, brilliant street of Moontown toward one of the big outfitting warehouses. Wandering, begging Titanians skipped hastily out of its way. Drunken space sailors and prospectors barely avoided its wheels. Yet the unearthly flood of green light that poured down from Uranus' huge hanging sphere lent an unreal beauty to the sordid place.

At the warehouse, Berdeau bargained keenly for the equipment. The main part of it was the eight massive anti-heaters for the ship. They looked like big silver cylinders. The outer shell encased powerful apparatus which, when fed power from cyclotrons, would radiate a continuous damping force that neutralized and destroyed the vibrations of radiant heat.

The ten heavy insulite suits had smaller anti-heaters fastened between the shoulders. The suits looked not un-like ordinary spacesuits, except that they were of a laminated material embodying the most heat-resistant materials available. Wearing one of them, a man could walk in heat that would otherwise destroy him.

WHEN they had the heavy, expensive equipment stowed in the rocket-truck, Berdeau ordered Lenning to drive to the spaceport.

"I know you'll be wanting to get away as soon as possible," the gambler said to North. "I'll be waiting for you to come back with my share of that Levium."

John North felt a certain relaxing of his uneasiness. It seemed that his vague suspicions of Berdeau had been without foundation.

The rocket-truck left Moontown and started along the short road that led through the jungle to the spaceport. On either side of them, the weird fern forest towered in green gloom. A big moon-bat swooped down into the path of their lights, and flashed startledly up again on flapping wings.

They were near the spaceport when John North glimpsed a figure in the road ahead. He exclaimed suddenly, and Lenning pulled up.

"What's the matter? Who is that?" Berdeau asked sharply. He and his men had drawn the atom-pistols they all wore at their belts.

"It's Steenie," North said worriedly, jumping down from the truck. "One of our crew—he's space-struck, and shouldn't be wandering here alone."

Steenie's vacant blue eyes were blinking against the rocket-truck's lamps when North and the others reached his side.

"Is that you, Johnny?" asked the space-struck sailor relievedly. "I'm glad it's you. I was going to go look for you, only I didn't know where to look."

And Steenie gestured wonderingly to the solemn, buzzing fern jungle that rose around them in the viridescent glow of huge Uranus.

"Haven't I been on this world before, Johnny? It seems to me I was here once before, a long time ago."

"Sure, you were here years ago, Steenie," North told him soothingly. "Don't you remember, when you were Wenzi's chief pilot?"

"I was a pilot once, wasn't I?" Steenie said eagerly. "They said I was the greatest space pilot of them all."

"You were that," North told him. "But you shouldn't be wandering around here alone, Steenie. Come On back to the *Meteor* with us."

Steenie's vacant eyes became troubled. "No, we can't go back to the ship Johnny. That's why I was going to look for you. The other men have the ship now."

"The other men? What other men?" Connor demanded alarmedly.

Steenie made a vague gesture. "The other men, in gray uniforms."

"Company men!" The dismayed exclamation exploded from John North's lips. "Young Sidney and his men have seized the *Meteor!*"

"How the devil would they take your ship if your pals were on guard as you said?" Berdeau's hissing voice demanded.

Steenie explained with childlike simplicity. "It was just a little while ago, Johnny. Whitey said I could go outside if I didn't go far from the ship. I wanted to look around. I was trying to remember if I hadn't been on this world before, back when I was a pilot—"

"Yes, but what did the men in gray do?" North brought him back to his tale. "How did they get into the *Meteor?*"

"I saw the men in gray going toward our ship," Steenie said earnestly. "They shot things that *popped* around the ship's door. Whitey and the others there went to sleep. Then the men in gray went into the ship. I was afraid to go there then. I thought I'd try to find you."

"Sleep-gas!" North said fiercely. "Sidney and his men used sleep-gas pellets to take the ship."

"WE'LL soon take it back from them," flamed Connor. The Irishman's heavy atom-pistol jumped into his hand. "Come on, Johnny—we'll blast those damned Company thugs right out of our way!"

"Wait a minute," North said urgently. "We can't do anything that way. There's only two of us—"

Charles Berdeau's quick voice interrupted. The gambler's handsome face was wolf-tense in the green planet-light.

"There's *six* of us in this, North. We'll help you recapture your ship."

North was amazed. "You're willing to buck the Company?"

Berdeau's white teeth gleamed. "Why not? I've got twenty thousand invested in your expedition, and a fortune to win if you succeed. I'm not going to see you fail."

"Ah, that's talking!" exulted Connor. "Why, the six of us can wipe up this moon with them."

"Take it easy," rapped North. "We don't want bloodshed. Maybe we can retake the *Meteor* without it."

They cut off the lights of the rocket-truck, and started on along the road through the fern jungle. At the edge of the spaceport, they stopped the vehicle and advanced around the edge of the spaceport to reconnoiter on foot.

Concealed by the shadow of the fern jungle edge, they studied the scene a hundred yards away. The *Meteor* lay where they had left it, light spilling from its open door. But now a trio of gray-uniformed men armed with atom-pistols stood watchfully outside the door.

"I can't understand Sidney's seizing the ship," North muttered. "I was sure his orders would be to trail us to Oberon."

"Come on, and we'll rush 'em," Connor said, his voice low, yet fierce.

"We can pick them off from right here," Berdeau said callously.

"Wait—we don't want unnecessary bloodshed," John North said rapidly. "If I could get into the ship secretly, and surprise them—"

"How the devil can you get into the *Meteor* secretly?" Connor demanded. "There's only one door, and they're standing right in it."

North turned quickly to Berdeau.

"Have you got a chainwrench in that rocket-truck? One big enough to take out a rocket-tube with?"

"I see your idea," Connor replied, his eyes lighting up. "Maybe you could get into the ship that way."

Charles Berdeau was frowning. "Yes, there's a kit of tools in the truck. But I don't understand—"

"You wait here, all of you," North told them tensely. "I'm going to get into the *Meteor* my own way. If I succeed in taking them by surprise, I'll signal you to come on."

"Is there going to be a fight, Johnny?" Steenie asked wonderingly.

But North was already slipping back through the shadow of the jungle toward the rocket-truck. He rummaged in its tool-locker until he found the heavy chain-wrench used for dismounting defective rocket-tubes. With it, and a smaller wrench, he started on his mission.

North circled around the edge of the spaceport, keeping in the deep shadow of the tall fern jungle, until he was on the other side of the *Meteor* from the door. Then he bolted out across the level ground, through the green glow of great Uranus, running softly and swiftly until he reached the shadows at the tail of the looming ship.

He crouched, listening. He could hear a dim murmur of voices from the Company men on guard at the ship door. But they could not see him, back here at the tail. The men were intently guarding the door that was the only entrance to the ship.

BESIDE NORTH, there projected the big tail rocket-tubes of the craft. There were sixteen of the massive tubes, each of them two feet in diameter. North rapidly fastened his chainwrench around the lowest tube. Then he paused, before commencing to unscrew the tube.

This was the danger point, he knew. The tube was bound to make a noise as it began to unscrew. North hesitated uncertainly. As he paused, he noticed that amid the low medley of jungle sounds there was the screeching scream of a moon-bat, regularly repeated, quite loudly.

North timed the interval of the moon-bat's rhythmic calls. He braced himself, gripping the chain-wrench. And just as the moon-bat screamed again, he exerted all his strength to twist the rocket-tube. The tube unscrewed a little with a sharp grating sound as the moon-bat called.

North crouched tense. But there was no alarm from the guards at the door. They had not heard. Breathing more easily, he unscrewed the rocket-tube with infinite care. He had a bad moment when it finally came free. The weight of the massive tube was such that he had to strain every muscle to lower it to the ground without making a betraying thud.

Removal of the tube had left an opening of two feet in diameter in the stubby tail of the *Meteor*. North reached inside it, into the flame-blackened power-pipe that had led to the tube. He unbolted the flange of the pipe and in a few moments had a section of it lifted out.

Dropping the tools, he crawled in through the opening. He stood in the dark cyc-room at the stern of the *Meteor*. Around him dimly loomed the massive cyclotrons and the labyrinthine maze of power-pipes, feed-lines and control lines. North drew his atom-pistol, and started softly forward through the ship.

He heard voices from the main cabin. He stepped silently along the narrow catwalk, and peered tautly into the long, lighted compartment.

CHAPTER SIX
Death in the "Meteor"

THE first thing he saw was that Whitey Jones and Dorak and Hansen sat on the floor against the wall, their hands and feet tightly bound. Whitey's single arm was lashed against his body. The massive face of the shock-headed blond giant was crimson with rage.

Aline Laurel stood erect and unbound. Her fine face was white with fury as she confronted Philip Sidney. The gray-uniformed young Company officer, his back toward North, was speaking earnestly to the girl.

"But I really seized the ship for your sake, Miss Laurel," Sidney implored. "I couldn't see a girl like you go to a horrible death on Thunder Moon in this chimerical expedition."

"Do you expect me to believe that?" Aline demanded, her dark eyes flashing. "After all that your Company has done to cheat us?"

Sidney made a helpless shrugging gesture. "Please believe me," he pleaded. "The fact is that the Company ordered me to let you all go on to Oberon, to follow you there and wait until you had the levium before we attacked you. But I couldn't let you go to that hellish moon."

North stepped swiftly and softly forward and jammed his atom-pistol into the young officer's back.

"Don't make a move, Sidney," he rasped. "Just raise your hands and don't call to your men outside…"

Sidney's arms shot up startledly. Incredulous amazement was replaced by sharp joy on Aline's white face.

"John North..." she exclaimed in a soft, low voice. "But how—"

"Johnny, they were waiting here for you and Mike to get back," Whitey was saying excitedly. "They got us with sleep-gas pellets."

"I know," North said. "This is what they used to do it with."

He had been searching Sidney's pockets, keeping his weapon jammed against the other's back. And in one jacket pocket he had found a stubby little pellet-gun with a magazine of sleep-gas pellets.

"Aline, untie Whitey and the others," John North said swiftly. "Sidney, you back against the wall. You take care of him, Whitey."

Philip Sidney backed against the wall, and turned to face North. The young officer's clean-cut face was flushed with anger, but he did not resist being tied.

"I've got to take care of the men at the door," North whispered. "Wait here, all of you—"

Gripping the little pellet gun, North crept along the catwalk to the airlock chamber of the door. The three Company men still stood watchfully in the opening, peering alertly out into the green-lit night.

North sighted the pellet gun and triggered rapidly. The almost silent hiss of compressed air drove the pellets of the weapon whizzing. The pellets hit the heads and shoulders of the three Company men, and exploded with a *whoosh* of magically expanding white vapor.

The Company men started an alarmed turning movement, but never completed it. They crumpled and collapsed as that super-anesthetic white vapor entered their nostrils.

North dragged their prostrate bodies clear of the ship and then waved his arm in urgent signal.

"Connor…Berdeau…" he called in a low voice. "All clear. Bring the stuff here at once."

HE HEARD them start the rocket-truck. Running without lights, it came rattling across the green-lit space-port toward the *Meteor*.

North went back quickly into the main cabin. Sidney had been tied into one of the space chairs.

"We've got to get off this moon at once," North rapped. "There are other Company officers here. They'll come to investigate."

"What about the anti-heater equipment?" Whitey cried.

"It's coming now," North replied. He told them in a few rapid sentences of his deal with Charles Berdeau. "Is that all right, Aline? I mean, offering Berdeau ten percent of the levium?"

"Of course!" she cried joyfully. "That solves our biggest difficulty—getting the anti-heat equipment."

Philip Sidney spoke up from the space chair in which he was tied. The young officer addressed himself to North.

"So now you've tied up with Charles Berdeau, the biggest scoundrel that's never been hung in the Solar System," the young officer said scathingly. His eyes snapped. "North, you're doing a criminal thing if you take this girl to Thunder Moon."

"You're just trying to stop us so you can get the levium for your Company," Aline charged hotly.

"Believe me, Miss Laurel, I'm thinking of your safety," Sidney said earnestly. "This whole venture to Thunder

Moon is madness. But if North and the others must go, they should at least leave you here."

North reluctantly admitted to himself that Sidney was sincere. He could see that the young Company officer had conceived more than a passing admiration for Aline Laurel.

"He's really right, Aline," North muttered troubledly. "You ought to stay here while we go on to Oberon."

"I won't do it, and I don't want any argument about it," the girl declared with unexpected firmness.

Connor stuck his frog-like face excitedly into the main cabin, with Charles Berdeau and Steenie behind him.

"Fine work, Johnny," exulted the Irishman. "Ah, this is a night to make up for all those dull, dead months on Earth…"

North rapidly introduced Berdeau. The gambler's black eyes ignored the others but rested with unconcealed appreciation on the girl.

"I didn't know I was to have such a charming business partner, Miss Laurel," he said, white teeth flashing in a smile. "If I'd known—"

North interrupted urgently. "We've got to get that equipment aboard in a hurry. Every minute our ship remains here is dangerous."

"I'll have Lenning and the boys bring the stuff in," Berdeau replied coolly. He strode back outside.

"Whitey, see that they put the stuff in the cyc-room where we can hook it up quickly," North sweated. "I've got to replace that rocket-tube I took out of the tail. Connor, you can help me."

HE HURRIED out. Lenning and Berdeau's other two men were already beginning to carry the massive anti-heaters into the ship.

North hastened back to the tail of the *Meteor*. He rapidly replaced the feed-pipe flange, and then he and Connor lifted the heavy rocket-tube back into place and started to screw it in.

As he tightened the tube with the chain-wrench, North heard them carrying the last of the heavy anti-heaters aboard. At that moment someone grabbed his arm.

He turned in a flash, dropping the wrench to snatch out his atom-pistol. But it was not, as he had expected, a Company man who had stolen upon him in the shadows. It was a small, white figure—a girl in a scanty synthesilk dress whose face was a strained white blur in the dark.

"Sailor, I came here to warn you," her low voice hurried. "You wouldn't stop to listen back there in the Pleasure Palace—"

"Nova Smith..." North was astounded, then angry. "What the devil do you mean by following us?"

The star-girl gripped his arm more tightly. "Sailor, *listen!* Berdeau's planning to double-cross you. I heard him talking to Lenning and the others there in the Pleasure Palace. He's planning to jump you and your friends before you leave here. He doesn't mean to let you go without him. He wants all that levium for himself..."

"The girl's space-struck!" Connor gasped. "It doesn't make sense."

"I tell you, it's true!" Nova said fiercely. "You did me a big favor tonight and I wanted to warn you. You wouldn't stop to listen so I followed you out here—waited till I saw a chance to speak to you out of Berdeau's hearing—"

All John North's suppressed suspicion of Berdeau flared into flame on the instant. He had been puzzled all along by the gambler's surprisingly cooperative attitude, but had thought there was no chance of trickery.

North's atom-pistol was in his hand. He told Connor swiftly, "Mike, come with me. You stay here, Nova."

At that moment came the blasting crash of an atom-gun, echoing muffledly from inside the *Meteor*. Then a sharp scream; a furious shout.

"Hell, we're too late!" swore Connor, plunging wildly forward.

North was ahead of him as they reached the door of the ship. They burst in to the main cabin, ready to trigger their weapons.

But North stopped, appalled. Hansen lay on the floor, his breast blackened by the fatal blast of an atom-gun. Whitey and Dorak, their faces livid, had their hands up.

Charles Berdeau faced North from behind Aline. The gambler had his atom-pistol leveled at the girl's back.

"You too, North!" snapped Berdeau. "Drop those guns and raise your hands or the girl gets a blast in the back…"

There was no possible reply to that threat. Slowly, trembling with fury, North and Connor dropped their weapons.

NORTH heard a sharp gasp of horror from behind him. Nova Smith had followed them into the ship. Berdeau's flaring eyes glimpsed the star-girl.

"So you came to warn them, Nova?" he rasped. "You'll regret that. Stand over there beside them. None of you try anything, or you'll get what this pal of yours on the floor got for resisting."

Lenning and Kells were hastily taking the weapons of North and his friends. Darm, Berdeau's third man, stood at the end of the cabin his atom-pistol reinforcing the gambler's commands.

Connor was still staring incredulously at Hansen's dead body on the floor. The Irishman was muttering frozenly.

"They killed Hansen," Connor said, unbelievingly. "Hansen, that sailed beside me for thirty years. Why, they can't do that. Why—"

The berserk look came into Connor's raging eyes. Berdeau saw it and yelled a warning.

"You and the girl both get it if you try anything."

No threat to himself could have penetrated Connor's blood-madness and halted him. But the threat to Aline stopped him.

He choked. His voice was a shaking whisper. "Berdeau, I'll kill you for this."

North saw Philip Sidney watching with wide, horrified eyes from the space chair in which he was bound. At that moment, Steenie came wandering into the cabin from the cyc-room.

"Johnny, can I pilot the ship a little when we start?" Steenie asked eagerly. "You know, I used to be a good pilot—"

His voice trailed off into silence as his vacant blue eyes fastened puzzledly on Hansen's body. "Somebody's hurt Hansen," he said, childlike distress in his voice. "Who was it hurt Hansen?"

With a contemptuous, brutal sweep of his arm, the hulking Lenning sent Steenie crashing back against the wall.

"Now listen to me, all of you," Berdeau's voice rasped. "We're going to Oberon after that levium. But *I* am running the expedition now."

North's blood was pounding in his temples. But he forced himself to speak steadily.

"Berdeau, the two girls can't help you get the levium. At least leave them here."

"I'm leaving no one here to set the Company or others on my trail," rapped the gambler. He glanced viciously at the star-girl. "Especially Nova, whom I owe something for trying to wreck my plans."

Nova Smith's small figure stiffened angrily, and there was no fear on her pert, painted face as she jerked her blonde head.

"I'm only sorry I wasn't in time to queer the whole thing," she defied the gambler.

"As for Miss Laurel," rasped Berdeau, "she's my ace card. Neither I nor my men can pilot a spaceship. But you men can, North. And you're going to do it for me. You're going to do it, because Lenning is going to keep a gun on Miss Laurel every minute. And at the first sign of disobedience or mutiny from any of you, an atom-blast will spoil her beauty."

ALINE LAUREL spoke to North. There were tears still glimmering in her dark eyes but her voice was level.

"I'm not afraid, John," she said. "You do what you think is best and pay no attention to his threats against me."

But North realized that he was checkmated. Bitterly as they longed to avenge Hansen's death, they could not attempt it when their first move would condemn Aline.

He spoke in a low voice to Whitey and Connor and Dorak. "He's got us boxed, boys. We'll have to do as he says."

"Now you are showing sense," Berdeau applauded ironically. The gambler laughed softly as his black eyes mockingly swept their livid faces. "Hard to take, isn't it?

But you senile old-timers ought to have known better than to come to space again. The frontier's too tough for you, these days."

Then Berdeau said harshly, "Miss Laurel, I want the written directions your father left for finding the levium. Hand them over, or I'll have Lenning search you for them."

Furiously, Aline thrust the scrap of yellowed paper at him. The gambler's black eyes were bright as he glanced at the scrawled writing.

Then he told her, "You take that space chair there. Lenning, sit across from her and keep her covered every minute. The rest of you prepare to take off at once. North, you'll pilot the ship."

The man Darm dragged Hansen's body outside and closed the ship's door. Connor went back to start the cycs, Kells going watchfully with him.

The gambler motioned North toward the control room, and followed him there. As North slowly took the pilot-chair, Berdeau strapped into the copilot seat beside him. He held his atom-pistol ready for action in his hand.

"Take off for Oberon at once," he ordered curtly. "I needn't warn you not to try any tricks, North. You know the consequences."

Helpless to disobey, North took the space-stick. His throat was dry, his whole body shaking with raging emotion.

"Blasting off!" he called hoarsely back into the ship.

He jammed the cyc-pedal to the floor.

The old *Meteor* bounded upward through the green planet-light with a roar of rocket-tubes.

They slanted up over the green-lit jungles of Titania. The scream of splitting air died rapidly outside as the old cruiser climbed to clear space. The huge bulk of cloudy green Uranus loomed on their left.

Less than a hundred thousand miles outward from them marched the sullen crimson sphere of Thunder Moon. The ship started blasting steadily toward it, its cycs droning loud and the tail tubes thundering.

North felt dazed by this wreck of all their hopes. This last space venture of himself and his aging comrades was ending in disaster. Peters and Hansen were dead. And Berdeau and his criminals commanded their ship as they rushed on toward the most perilous spot in the System.

CHAPTER SEVEN
Thunder Moon!

THE outermost satellite of Uranus was unique among the moons of the Solar System. It was not large, this moon Oberon that had received such forbidding name and fame. It was little more than a thousand miles in diameter, and its small mass should long ago have cooled to quiescence like the other satellites.

But Oberon had never cooled, never since the day when it and its parent world had been flung off by the Sun. Much of its mass had solidified, but beneath that solid crust raged unquenchable internal fires forever fed by a too-great radioactive content of its core. Flames from its fiery heart burst ceaselessly through rifts and craters in the crust, and fountained up from the surging molten rock of the Flaming Ocean.

Wrapped in its gloomy, smoky haze, the volcanic moon was an ever more appalling spectacle as the *Meteor* drew toward it, hour by hour. North had kept their speed throttled down, stretching out the traverse as long as possible. His mind was still feverishly searching for some means of turning the tables on Berdeau and his men.

But North could think of nothing. The gambler, from the copilot seat, watched his every move. And the first sign of mutiny, North knew, would seal Aline Laurel's death warrant. He dared attempt nothing until a better opportunity presented on the dangerous moon they were now approaching.

North spoke tautly to the man beside him. "It's time we hooked up those anti-heaters. We'll need them going every minute we're on Oberon."

Berdeau's black eyes narrowed. "All right, North—you can call one of your pals to take the controls while you hook them up."

Dorak came forward to relieve North.

The stolid spaceman's eyes glanced toward Berdeau with open hate, but he said nothing as he took over.

North's gaze flew anxiously to Aline as he went back into the main cabin. She was pale, but there was a courageous lift to her chin. Sidney, sitting in the space chair next to her, was talking to her earnestly. The hulking Lenning had his atom-pistol on his knee, trained directly at her. And one of Berdeau's two other men watched alertly from the end of the cabin.

"I'm all right, John," Aline said in answer to North's wordless inquiry.

"She's not all right—she's in deadly danger, and it's your fault," Philip Sidney said bitterly to North. "You just had to bring her, didn't you?"

"That's not true—I insisted on coming," Aline said indignantly.

But North himself made no answer. He felt heavily that the young Company officer's accusation was only too justified.

He looked around. "Where's Nova?"

"Back in my cabin," Aline informed. "I lent her a jacket and slacks—she couldn't wear that dance costume of hers here."

North motioned to Whitey. "I've got to go back and hook up the anti-heaters. We'll soon reach Oberon. I'll need your help."

Lenning, watching and listening, spat an order to the hard-faced young man on guard at the end of the cabin. "Go with them, Darm."

As North shouldered back along the narrow catwalk to the cyc-room with Whitey, he muttered under his breath to the one-armed giant.

"If we could dig out an atom-pistol and blast that brute Lenning before he could harm Aline—"

"No chance, Johnny," murmured Whitey Jones. "Darm and Kells went through the whole ship for weapons. They've got us cold."

"No whispering, you two," snarled the man Darm, behind them.

BACK in the crowded cyc-room, which was shuddering to the thunderous droning roar of the massive cyclotrons, they found Connor glaring silently at the third criminal, Kells.

They set to work to hook up the big anti-heaters to the cycs. Darm and Kells watched them closely. Yet as they stooped to fasten the power-feed lines, North found an opportunity to whisper to Connor.

"Don't start anything yet, Mike. Our chance will come when we reach Thunder Moon."

Connor's whisper was hoarse with passion. "Don't any of you kill Lenning when the time comes. He's mine. I found out he shot Hansen."

They started the big anti-heaters, turning the power into them. The massive mechanisms began a pulsing throb. A halo of blue force burgeoned out from them—a dim nimbus surrounding the flying *Meteor*. It was the damping force that could effectually neutralize radiant heat.

"That ought to keep the worst of the heat out," North muttered.

He started back forward. Nova Smith met him in the narrow catwalk. North stared wonderingly at the star-girl.

The soft gray space-jacket and slacks had changed her outward appearance. Even more transformation had been wrought by the fact that she had scrubbed away the garish paint on her face and combed her yellow hair smoothly back.

"Don't look so surprised, sailor," she told North a little resentfully. "You didn't think I *liked* wearing all that stuff on my face, did you? But a star-girl has to dress the part."

"You shouldn't have tried to warn me, Nova," he said gloomily. "It only got you into trouble yourself."

"Sailor, I've been in trouble half my life," she replied with a gamin grin. "That cheap crook Berdeau doesn't scare me any."

"Move along, you two," snarled Kells warningly behind them.

North shouldered forward through the cabin toward the control room. Steenie touched his arm anxiously to delay him a moment.

"Can I pilot the ship a little now, Johnny?" Steenie asked eagerly for the hundredth time. "You know, I was a good pilot once."

"I know, and we'll let you pilot some time soon," North told him hastily. "You go back now and be quiet, Steenie."

Dorak rose to yield him the pilot-chair. "Take over again, Johnny. We'll be landing soon, and my eyes aren't good enough for that."

Thunder Moon now filled half the sky with its crimson, haze-wrapped sphere. They saw its atmosphere as a roiling gloom of smoke, shot through with red lightings of bursting fires beneath.

North was wire-taut as he began to edge the *Meteor* around in a closing spiral, into the smoky atmosphere. He called back to those in the cabin to strap in, as they spiraled toward the volcanic moon.

Far around the curve of the moon, he spotted the steady red glow in the haze that marked the location of the Flaming Ocean. He slanted the ship in that direction. The rising scream of parting atmosphere crawled at his nerves. He strained his eyes tensely to peer through the drifting smoke.

Berdeau, looking at the yellowed paper he had taken from Aline, spoke harshly, "The basalt plateau old Laurel mentioned must be the only safe landing-place. Be sure we land there, North—or we all die together."

"I know," rapped John North. "I've no desire to kill my friends."

His mind feverishly repeated Thorn Laurel's written directions.

"Levium deposit in west one of three crater peaks rising from Flaming Ocean. Landing possible only on basalt plateau near spear-shaped bay on south coast… Use stone raft to cross Ocean to peaks. Look out for the Fieries."

NORTH could see almost nothing through the roiling smoke beneath—nothing but occasional geysers of flame from volcanic rifts. The descending *Meteor* shuddered wildly from impact of shattering vibrations in the smoky haze. The crashes of thunder that had given Oberon its name were each few moments drowning out the roar of the cycs and staccato detonation of the rockets.

A huge glow pulsed down there in the haze ahead. The clouds of smoke seemed thinner above it, due to the atmospheric currents. The ship dived unsteadily down into that area of thinner haze. Below lay a vast sea of evilly crimson lava, upon whose wave-less surface danced changing flames.

They were plunging toward the dreaded Flaming Ocean of Thunder Moon. North frantically jerked the space-stick, cutting in keel and lateral rockets to swing them southward. But the ferocious atmospheric currents above this hell-sea of molten rock batted the *Meteor* about like a leaf in a storm.

He fought the ship's nose around and jammed the cyc-pedal to the floor. The old craft leaped with a gallant surge of power, struggling southward over the molten expanse. Then, far to westward, North glimpsed three steep crater peaks whose black pinnacles rose sheer from the red lava.

"There—the three craters!" yelled Charles Berdeau, treasure-lust flaming in his eyes.

No ship could land on the precipitous slopes of those towering peaks, North knew. He flung the lurching *Meteor* toward the distant southern shore of the flaming sea.

"Look for that spear-shaped bay," he ordered hoarsely.

The continent south of the Flaming Ocean rushed toward them. It was a nightmare spectacle under the fire-shot pall of smoke. A tumbled wilderness of upheaved rocks smoking fiercely in the terrific heat, its infernal rivers were red-blazing streams of living lava flowing down to the molten sea from the fiery springs in which they spouted to the surface. Farther southward, a range of great volcanoes were jetting clouds of ashes.

North's eyes desperately searched the coast of the infernal continent but saw no indentation of spear-like shape. He twitched the space-stick to turn the ship westward along the shore of the molten sea. But the screaming currents of the smoke spun the *Meteor* dizzily upward, the crash of its lateral rocket-tubes only serving to send it farther out of control.

Hoarse, bellowing thunder in the smoky haze about them seemed to mock North's frantic efforts to right the plunging craft. At perilously low altitude, he got it back on something like even keel, and drove it west along the burning coast with the full blast of its tail tubes.

"There's the bay!" yelled Berdeau, pointing. "But where in hell's name is the basalt plateau?"

North had glimpsed the deep, narrow indentation in the shore at the same moment as the gambler.

He sent the ship plunging recklessly down through the roiling smoke. His eyes were fiercely searching the smoking shore of the bay. Then he saw the long, slightly upraised ledge of black basalt that lay almost a mile from the molten sea.

"There it is—but it's terribly small to land a ship on in these currents," North exclaimed.

THE *Meteor* was rushing headlong down toward the fiery coast. North's eyes, tensely estimating distances through the billowing smoke, perceived that they would fall short of the basalt ledge.

He frantically kicked all the power of the cycs into the keel-tubes. The jerk of the downward blast kept the ship from losing altitude for a moment longer, as it plunged screaming through the smoke.

Hellish clouds of rushing black vapor obscured the window for a terrible second. Bawling of thunder in the haze about them derided them. Then screaming currents tore the blinding smoke away from in front.

"You've overshot it!" Berdeau shouted thinly over the uproar.

The *Meteor* was plunging down past the narrow basalt ledge toward the river of blazing lava that flowed along its southward side.

North's hands jerked the space-stick with blurring speed and his foot thrust and eased and thrust again on the cyc-pedal in a split-second.

Crash! Crash-crash! The ship stood on its tail from the mad blast of its rockets, rolled back over and spun to the laterals, and then sagged toward the basalt ledge on the flaming columns of its keel-jets. A jarring bump, a screech of scraping metal—and they had landed.

"By God, you're a pilot, North…" swore Berdeau.

Then the gambler gestured meaningly with his atom-pistol. "Now get back into the cabin with the others."

North felt limp and shaky from reaction as he unstrapped. It had taken every ounce of his spacemanship to achieve that precarious landing.

In the main cabin, the others were peering through the windows in fascinated awe, Berdeau's men still watching them closely. Drifting smoke veiled most of the infernal scene outside. But the parked ship was shuddering every few moments to the bawling crash of thunder. And its interior was uncomfortably warm despite the protective nimbus of the anti-heaters.

"What a terrible world," whispered Aline Laurel.

"It's sure no summer resort," declared Nova. "I thought we were goners when we started to fall toward that fiery ocean."

"That was a wonderful landing, North," said young Philip Sidney with warm admiration. "Whoever taught you piloting knew his business."

North answered haggardly, "The greatest pilot that ever flew space taught me. There he is, over there—what's left of him."

And he nodded toward Steenie, who sat staring out at the smoke-veiled scene with childish wonder in his vacant blue eyes.

Charles Berdeau appeared in the cabin door. Connor jumped to his feet, and Whitey Jones' massive figure stiffened. But the gambler's black eyes swept their hostile faces coolly. He spoke crisply.

"It's time you all understood the situation clearly," Berdeau rasped. "I want that levium deposit and I mean to have it. But I don't want to have to kill any of you, unless you make it necessary."

"Big-hearted Charlie, they called him back on Titania," cracked Nova Smith.

Berdeau shot the star-girl an ugly glance but went on evenly. "Now listen to reason. We've got the atom-guns and there's nothing you can do. This world is dangerous, and the sooner we get off it, the safer you'll all be. Cooperate with us, and I'll promise to give you a tenth share of the levium when we get back."

"What kind of 'cooperation' do you want from us?" North demanded.

THE gambler explained. "It's not going to be easy to get out to those crater peaks in the Ocean and get the levium. We'll need help. Give us that help without starting a fight, and you'll all profit by it."

"We'll see you damned before we help you and your filthy killers," flamed Connor.

Whitey nodded his massive blond head in grim agreement. "If it wasn't for that gun covering Aline, we'd be at your throat now, Berdeau."

But North had been thinking. The thin edge of a desperate idea had entered his mind. If he could find a chance for the risky stratagem—

"What's the use, boys?" North said heavily to his comrades. "They have us cold. We have no other choice than to do as they say."

They stared at him unbelievingly. Dorak asked incredulously, "You mean we should do what these murderers ask?"

"What else can we do?" John North countered in a hopeless voice.

Nova Smith's blue eyes flashed at North. "Sailor, don't be foolish," said the star-girl. "Can't you see that Berdeau will only put you all out of the way as soon as he's safe back on Titania with the levium?"

"I've warned you before about talking too much, Nova," flared the gambler. "Another word out of you—"

John North knew that the star-girl had told the truth. He knew quite well that Berdeau would use them to help him secure the levium and pilot him back to Titania, and then would dispose of them swiftly.

But he shrugged helplessly. "We've got to do as they say," he repeated. "If we don't, it means Aline's life."

Connor and Whitey and Dorak gave in, at that reminder. Their fierce silence as they faced Berdeau was confession of defeat.

"Now you're being sensible," the gambler approved coolly. Then he gave his orders. "North, you and Connor will go out with Lenning and me in a preliminary reconnaissance. The first job is to figure out a way to get out across the Flaming Ocean to those craters."

The gambler added, "Darm, you and Kells will remain on guard here. Remember to watch Miss Laurel every minute."

North's heart was beating with a steady, suppressed excitement as he hurriedly got out four of the insulite suits. The suits weren't that different from ordinary spacesuits, except that the stiff black material they were fashioned from served as a far heavier insulation; and their helmets were massive, opaque ones with only an eye-slit in front. Each had its own oxygenator and standard short-radius space-suit phone.

Berdeau and Lenning got into the garments first, and then North and Connor. They started the individual anti-heaters attached to the shoulders of the suits. Each of them was at once shrouded in a blue nimbus of heat-neutralizing force.

"Don't forget your moon-shoes," North warned, stooping to slip on his own heavy, lead-soled sandals. "Surface gravity here is low."

Berdeau and the hulking Lenning both carried their atom-pistols in their gloved hands as they opened the air-lock. North and Connor stepped into the airlock first at Berdeau's order.

"You two go first, North," ordered Berdeau. "And you will stay twenty feet in front of us at all times. Understand?"

North and the Irishman passed out through the airlock. They stepped onto the rough black basalt outside the parked ship.

Drifting clouds of black smoke swirled about them. Ashes were raining down upon them, pattering on their heavy helmets. And even through the heavy insulation of the suits and the protective nimbus of their anti-heaters, penetrated suffocating heat. They had stepped out into a temperature of hundreds of degrees.

CHAPTER EIGHT
Moon Monsters

THE basalt lurched and shuddered under their feet, as distant convulsions of the tortured fire-moon rocked its unstable crust. Each of those convulsive tremors was accompanied by an ear-splitting, echoing detonation, like the drumfire of heavy artillery.

Drum crashes of cosmic thunder that rocked and rolled and ebbed and then burst forth again! That hoarse hubbub of colossal reverberations through the fire-shot gloom crushed the mind by its sheer volume. Added to the suffocating heat and blinding smoke, it almost dazed North.

Berdeau's voice came to him on the spacesuit phone. The gambler sounded as though he also were a little stunned.

"Heavens…what a world," he was muttering.

He and Lenning had emerged from the ship. North turned toward them, and pointed through the smoke. "The Ocean lies this way."

"You two lead," ordered the gambler watchfully. "We'll follow."

And Berdeau and his hulking aide remained well behind North and Connor as they started forward through the smoky gloom.

North dared not attempt the precarious plan he had formed, so near the ship. His scheme was desperate to the last degree. Failure would cost not only their own lives, but probably Aline's also.

He trudged forward with Connor on the heavy moon-shoes, groping a way through the smoke. The rocking bursts of thunder from distant splitting rocks seemed louder than ever to his ringing ears. They were soon out of sight of the ship in the hazy gloom.

The heat was intense, even through the nimbus of protective force that shrouded his insulite suit. He knew that without his anti-heater, the suit could not protect him for a minute from these terrific temperatures.

Connor uttered a sharp exclamation of alarm and jerked North back. They had reached the west edge of the basalt plateau. They stood a few yards above a blazing river of molten red lava.

North understood they had veered in a wrong direction in the smoke, and he changed their course. Greater heat beat through his suit, and he glimpsed through the smoke at the pulsing crimson glow of the Flaming Ocean.

The two stood gazing petrifiedly, Berdeau and Lenning also gazing dazedly from a distance behind them. The spectacle was awesome. The great flood of molten crimson lava stretched before them to the horizon. Its red glow glared up into the sky. No wind could have stirred that heavy expanse of liquid rock, but the tidal pull of the parent planet caused long, surging swells that broke against the shore in fiery spray.

Far out in the Flaming Ocean rose the three steep black crater peaks. North's bleared, aching eyes estimated them at least three or four miles away. His heart beat faster as he looked on the westernmost of those three volcanic pinnacles that held the most fabulous treasure of the System.

Berdeau's voice came, raw with treasure-lust. "The levium's in that west crater. By Heaven, we've got to reach that peak somehow. North, wouldn't it be possible to get there with the ship?"

"Not in a million years," North retorted emphatically. "No pilot could land on these steep slopes, amid those hellish atmospheric currents."

"Old Laurel said to cross out on a stone raft," muttered the gambler. "But stone won't float on that molten lava, will it?"

North stooped and tossed a chunk of the black basalt out into the hissing flood. It sank from sight.

"This basalt won't float but there must be lighter rock," North said. "We'll have to find some."

They left the basalt ledge and moved over smoking rocks so hot that the lead soles of their moon-shoes began to soften and bulge. But this rock floated, when they cast a piece into the fiery sea.

"Good," exclaimed Berdeau. "We'll quarry a big block for a raft—"

"Johnny, *look!*" came Connor's wild warning. "To your right!"

North pitched around, and was stunned by incredulous horror. A half dozen vague, crouching shapes were approaching them through the smoke.

They were not men, nor did they wear any protective suits. They were monstrous creatures of the infernal moon, advancing to attack.

THE creatures were quadrupeds, and looked something like big baboons. But their bodies had a queer, metallic appearance. And indeed, no flesh of ordinary organic compounds could have existed for more than a minute in that tremendous heat.

The faces in the brutish heads had only two features—a gaping mouth of shining metal teeth, and wide-set, unchanging crystal eyes. The rear feet were hard metallic hoofs, but the front feet were massive, gleaming talons. Most terrifying of all, bursting flames issued from the mouths of the creatures at each exhalation.

Here, North knew, was a form of life infinitely far removed from the evolutionary line of ordinary planets. Here strange life that had stirred in metallic salts had developed to a semi-intelligent form. He guessed that the creatures dug raw mineral elements for their nutriment. That their bodies could consume such elements was evidenced by the fact that the chemical process of their tissues was one of continuous combustion.

Connor was shouting wildly. "They must be the Fieries that old Laurel warned about…"

North spun around toward Berdeau and Lenning, standing rooted in amazed horror some yards behind.

"Use your atom-guns!" North yelled. "Those things are going to attack. Mike, get back…"

Berdeau woke from his daze. He and Lenning leveled their heavy atom-pistols at the advancing Fieries and triggered hastily.

The crashing streaks of atomic flame hit the foremost Fieries—and splashed harmlessly off them. The concentrated blasts could no more than scorch those metallic bodies whose very life-process was one of fire.

"Good lord, atom-guns are no good against them!" came Lenning's hoarse, horrified cry.

"Back to the ship!" North shouted to the others. "They'll tear us to bits…"

The men turned and pitched through the smoke in the direction of the *Meteor*. But they could not sprint in the heavy moon-shoes, which alone made it possible to walk normally in this weak gravity. The Fieries came after them, running with shambling swiftness on four feet.

North heard a yell of horror from Lenning. He glanced back and saw that Lenning had stared too long in his petrified amazement, before starting to run. The Fieries had caught up to him. Their metallic bodies bore the hulking criminal to the ground.

But Connor too had been slow to retreat. Two of the grotesque creatures were gaining rapidly on the Irishman, North saw in his backward glance.

"Mike, look out!" North yelled frantically to the other, and started back.

The two Fieries overtook Connor as he shouted warning. They leaped upon his back. The powerful talons of one caught in the heavy insulite of his suit and ripped it.

Connor staggered as from sudden agony. "God—" choked his voice.

North had snatched up a loose chunk of basalt as he ran back to aid his comrade. Connor was off his feet, the two Fieries on him.

NORTH hammered madly with his chunk of stone at the two creatures. They recoiled from the furious blows, which apparently could hurt them where the atom-pistols had not.

He seized the opportunity to grab Connor by the belt and stumbled away with him through the smoke. Over on his left, North glimpsed the other four of the creatures clustered around Lenning's prone form, tearing his suit to ribbons. Lenning's body was already scorched and blackened by the terrific heat.

Berdeau was disappearing in the smoke ahead. North followed with frenzied haste, dragging and half-carrying Connor's limp form. The two Fieries had started to pursue him, then had darted to join the others who were tearing at Lenning's suit.

The massive bulk of the *Meteor* loomed out of the smoke. A louder crash of thunder from the distant volcanoes shook North almost from his feet. But he gained the airlock, and then collapsed on the floor as he got through it into the ship.

Berdeau was already stripping off his suit in there, Kells and Darm running alarmedly toward him with atom-guns ready for action.

"They got Lenning," Berdeau was saying, his white face beaded with sweat, his voice hoarse. "They tore his suit to bits—"

Whitey and Dorak were running forward to North. "Johnny, are you all right?" cried the one-armed giant.

North gasped for breath as he got the helmet off his head. "Help Mike!" he panted. "They punctured his suit—the heat got through—"

Dorak and Philip Sidney were already getting off Connor's helmet and suit. The Irishman lay, his battered face flushed dull, unnatural red, his breath coming in choking gurgles.

Nova Smith's small figure came flying to North's side. "Sailor, here's the medicine kit. His back is burned—"

Connor's back was more than burned—it was crisped black by the terrific heat that had entered through his punctured suit. North's heart stood still as he saw. The Irishman groaned a little under their touch.

Connor's eyes opened, moved with an effort over the white faces of those gathered over him. Words dribbled huskily from his mouth.

"No use, Johnny," he whispered. "I'm—done for. Getting cold—"

His eyes half-closed. "I'd—like a drink—"

It was Nova Smith who flew for the brandy bottle, and steadied it at his lips. Connor's hand dropped to the star-girl's shoulder. The ghost of his old grin hovered for a moment on his face.

"Way I always wanted to die," he whispered. "Holding a pretty girl and a bottle—"

The last word was a trailing sigh, as his mouth went slack and his eyes closed and his head rolled back.

ALINE LAUREL burst into sobs. Philip Sidney soothed her, his own face white and strained.

Nova looked at John North, winking back the tears in her blue eyes. "I know how you must feel, sailor—"

But North said nothing, only looking sickly at Whitey and Dorak and at Steenie, who was watching with puzzled wonder from a little distance.

A scraping of something against the outer hull of the ship broke the silence. A terrified cry came from Aline as they saw outside the windows the grotesque gray forms of a score of Fieries who were clawing at the ship with their talons in brutish wonder.

The man Kells exclaimed hoarsely, "Good lord, those devils are attacking the ship!"

Berdeau's sharp voice silenced him. "They're only the Fieries that old Laurel warned of. They're immune to atom-guns, but we've got to get rid of them somehow."

"If I turned on the cycs and gave them a blast out of the lateral rocket-tubes…" Philip Sidney suggested.

The gambler nodded. "Do that. Kells, go along with him."

In a few moments, came the staccato crash of the rockets. The brief spurt of flame from the side tubes of the ship sent the scrabbling Fieries recoiling hastily. They beat a hasty retreat through the smoke.

In dead silence, North and Whitey and Dorak wrapped Connor's body. Wearing the insulite suits, they took it outside for burial. Kells and Darm went along with their atom-guns grimly ready.

They raised a cairn of rocks over their dead comrade, some little distance from the ship. Then in unbroken silence they plodded back through the smoke to the *Meteor*.

Steenie looked at North puzzledly as he took off his helmet. "Isn't Mike coming back, Johnny?" asked the space-struck pilot.

"No, Steenie," North said dully. "Mike isn't coming back."

Aline broke into tears. "Let's get away from this terrible world before others die," she sobbed. "It took my father's life—it's taken scores of others—"

"We don't leave here until we get that levium."

Charles Berdeau's voice rang like steel, his atom-pistol cradled grimly in his hand as he stood sweeping them with masterful black eyes.

"There's a billion dollars worth of levium over in that crater in the Flaming Ocean," the gambler bit out. "I'm not quitting when a pot like that is within my reach."

North said in a slow, bitter voice, "Connor wouldn't have been killed if you hadn't had him come out with us, Berdeau."

"He was set to make trouble—I didn't dare leave him here in the ship," rapped Berdeau, his face taut. "There'll be no more trouble, unless you try to buck my orders."

Whitey's massive form was stiff with rage, his face flaring. But again North warned the one-armed giant with a glance to wait. Three atom-pistols would scythe down not only them but the two girls, if they brought things to a head here. North still fiercely clung to his precarious scheme.

"We're going after that levium now," Berdeau was snapping. "We're *all* going—all except the girls and that space-struck idiot. I'm leaving no one here who could take the ship and blast off and leave me marooned on this damned world."

"But if something happens to all of us out there, the girls will be unable to leave—will face slow death here…" protested Philip Sidney.

"That," rasped Berdeau, "will make you careful to see that nothing does happen. Get into your suits. We'll take along picks, bars and cables. We should be strong enough to beat back the Fieries if they attack again."

NORTH slowly started to put his insulite suit and helmet back on, and Sidney and Whitey Jones and Dorak followed his example.

"I want to go with you, sailor," announced Nova unexpectedly, to North. Her pert face was pale and anxious. "I could help you—"

North shook his head. "You've got to stay here with Aline and Steenie, Nova. We'll be back. Don't you worry about that."

They all had their suits on. Berdeau motioned them grimly to the airlock. He and his two criminals kept them covered, forcing them to lead the way outside.

Out there in the thunder-riven smoke, North looked swiftly around. There was no sign of the Fieries who had attacked them before. But he and his two old comrades and Sidney gripped their steelite picks more tightly as they started forward a good distance ahead of Berdeau's group.

The basalt plateau shuddered beneath their feet with each crashing detonation that reverberated through the smoke. Clouds of ashes continued to rattle off their helmets. They moved obliquely toward the right, leaving the basalt ledge as they approached the shore of the molten lava sea.

Berdeau, standing guard with his two men at a little distance, indicated a great flat mass of the lighter black rock at the shore of the lava ocean.

"That will float on the lava and it'll make a big enough raft to hold all of us," the iron-willed gambler declared. "North, you and Jones and Dorak start cutting it loose. Sidney, you cut some stone paddles."

They bent to the work, splitting the flat mass of rock away with their picks and bars, and then slowly prying it toward the crimson, hissing flood of lava a few feet away. Only the lower gravity of the moon made the task possible, and even so they had to strain every muscle.

"Fieries coming!" yelled Kells' voice suddenly, hoarse with panic.

A full dozen of the crouching, fire-breathing quadrupeds were shambling toward them from the east.

"Some of you drive them back with your picks!" Berdeau yelled. "The rest launch that raft!"

North and Dorak and Whitey met the rush of the charging Fieries with flailing picks and bars. North's pick shattered the crystal eyes or sense organs of one of the creatures that charged him. The creature groped blindly for him with furious talons.

Whitey had almost decapitated another of the metallic-bodied monsters with a whirling blow from his heavy bar. The Fieries recoiled from the fierce defense, for the moment.

"Onto the raft!" shouted Berdeau. "Quick, before they rush again."

Sidney and the criminal Kells had got the massive slab of black rock launched on the molten lava. Berdeau already stood on it, as it floated on the hissing flood, his pistol commanding the situation.

North and his two comrades leaped out after the others, landing on the rocking raft of stone. Darm leaped wildly after them.

"Paddle—quick!" Berdeau was yelling.

The Fieries were rushing toward the shore. The ponderous floating mass of stone slowly forged out onto the lava flood as North and his friends seized the stone paddles Sidney had cut, and worked them furiously.

The balked creatures bunched on the shore, glaring after them with the saucer-like crystalline eyes. Berdeau, standing with Darm and Kells on the front of the strange raft, pointed northward across the flaming sea.

"Keep her headed toward those three crater peaks."

NORTH almost admired the indomitable resolution of the gambler in that moment. Their situation was perilous in the extreme. A sliding current of the thick lava had seized the raft and threatened to carry it westward.

The heat that glared up from the crimson-glowing lava was almost overpowering, even through the protective nimbus of their anti-heaters and their thick suits. Each stroke of the stone paddles sent up showers of fiery spray behind them.

Yet the crude stone raft forged on northward over the flaming sea. The three steep crater peaks loomed larger ahead. But they seemed only creeping across that two-mile expanse.

Ashes continued to rattle down upon them from the range of volcanoes spouting tempests of fire in the far south. Clouds of smoke whirled down and enveloped them in a lurid darkness for moments. Around them and over them, threatening sometimes to tear them from the raft, screamed the ferocious atmospheric currents that rushed above the fiery sea.

"This—is hell itself," choked Philip Sidney, laboring with his paddle beside North. "We'll never get back with the levium over this."

Fierce storms of changing flames danced here and there on the surface of the lava flood. One such typhoon of fire glided toward them.

"Paddle to the west!" North yelled warningly. "Get out of the way of that firestorm!"

They hastily veered their course. And the tempest of bursting flames roared but a few dozen yards from them, passing southward.

Long, grinding detonations of diastrophism deep within the volcanic moon were followed by heaving waves of lava on which the raft rocked precariously. Yet they were getting closer now to the three craters.

North dug his stone paddle again, and again, and again, bending his head to the task. When he once more looked up, the westernmost of the three craters loomed full ahead.

It was not an active volcano, though it looked as though it had been so not long ago. It was a jagged black conical peak, rising sheer from the Flaming Ocean without any ledge or shelf along its base big enough for a spaceship to land. But there was one narrow shelf toward which they directed the stone raft, upon which men might leap ashore.

The stone raft bumped the shore. Berdeau and his two criminals were first ashore on the ledge, at once moving a safe distance of thirty feet away to cover the activities of the others with their weapons.

"Bring those picks and bars and cables with you," Berdeau was ordering harshly. "We'll moor the raft here with one of the cables."

Whitey and Sidney and Dorak stepped ashore with the tools. But North, as he stepped across the crude rock raft, stooped as though he had stumbled. His hands surreptitiously loosened the fastenings of his moon-shoes.

The time to essay his desperate stratagem had come. He knew he would be given but one chance.

He straightened, as though to shuffle on, off of the raft. But instead, his feet kicked off his leaden moon-shoes. And he bunched and sprang for Berdeau and the other two criminals.

The three were thirty feet away. But thirty feet through the air like a human projectile shot John North's figure, now that he had rid himself of the moon-shoes that had held him down against the weak gravity.

He heard Berdeau's gasping shout. "You *fool*—"

The crashing blast of the gambler's atom-pistol streaked toward North at the same instant. But he was moving too fast for the aim to be accurate. It grazed past his helmet the moment before he struck Berdeau.

He bore the gambler to the ground, fiercely gripping his gun-hand and at the same time thrusting his legs to trip Kells and Darm.

"Dorak...Sidney... Jump them—*now!*" he yelled.

CHAPTER NINE
In the Crater

NORTH heard the crash of an atom-gun close by as he struggled fiercely with Berdeau. Yells and a gasping gurgle of agony came to him on the spacesuit phone but he could not turn now to see who was hit.

Berdeau was fighting like a demon. North had twisted his arm until he dropped the atom-pistol, but the gambler was struggling to grab it again and he was on the point of succeeding.

North desperately put all his strength into a convulsive effort that sent Berdeau staggering backward. In the moment that followed, North snatched up the fallen atom-pistol and leveled it at the gambler.

"Stand back and keep your hands up or I'll blast you, Berdeau," he ordered in a steely voice.

The fight upon the narrow ledge was over. But that fierce, brief explosion of conflict had taken its toll.

The criminal Darm lay prone and unmoving, the glassite eye-slit of his helmet smashed and his face withering black from the heat. Whitey's giant form was straightening from the dead man.

Sidney had got Kells' pistol and was covering the other criminal. But Jan Dorak lay behind them, gripping his leg and gasping in agony.

"Darm got Dorak before I killed him," panted Whitey to North.

North let the other two cover Berdeau and Kells, while he stooped to Dorak's side. The stolid spaceman's leg had been hit by the crashing atom-blast, and his insulite suit had been torn through.

His face was contorted with agony inside his helmet, and he spoke to North through pain-clenched teeth.

"My leg—burning up," he gasped. "But I'm not hurt bad—"

North cut a square of insulite from the suit of the dead Darm and bound it tightly around Dorak's leg. It would keep the terrific heat from entering Dorak's suit for the time being.

Then they cut lengths from one of the steelite cables and bound the hands and feet of Berdeau and Kells. The gambler's eyes raged at North from inside his helmet's eye-slit as they finished.

North found himself shaking from reaction. He had hardly dared hope that his stratagem of attack would actually succeed.

"I didn't dare try that stunt before," he said hoarsely to Whitey and Sidney. "For always before, Berdeau had someone covering Aline and the first sign of attack would have meant her death."

"It was good work, Johnny," Whitey said warmly. "I was beginning to think you'd never act."

North looked up the steep slope of the crater peak at whose base they stood. The towering cone-shaped pinnacle was crusted over with solidified lava from past eruptions. There was a practicable path up its side that North's searching eyes traced out swiftly.

"Now for the levium," he said tautly. "Then we can get back to the *Meteor* and get away from this hellish moon."

He turned to Dorak, who lay back against the side of the ledge watching them with pain-narrowed eyes.

"Go ahead, fellows," muttered Dorak. "I can watch Berdeau and Kells while you're gone."

North gave him one of the atom-pistols. "Blast them if they try to move, Jan," he said.

But there seemed small possibility of Berdeau or Kells attempting escape, since they lay bound hand and foot upon the narrow ledge. Berdeau had not uttered a word since this sudden reversal of fortune. The gambler was taking it with the cool imperturbability that characterized him.

THEY moored their stone raft to the ledge with one of the cables. And then, carrying the rest of the cables and most of the picks and bars, they started up the side of the towering cone."

North led the way, seeking to tallow the tentative path his eyes had marked out up the lava ledges and cracks of the mighty crater. But it was a narrow, dangerous trail— made more precarious by the continual rumbling convulsions of Thunder Moon, which shook the whole crater peak.

Black clouds of smoke swooped down on them like giant bats, to shroud them in momentary darkness. The screaming atmospheric currents seemed stronger up here than below, and threatened to tear them bodily from their precarious footholds. Hundreds of feet beneath them smoldered the crimson, molten expanse of the Flaming Ocean.

North's mind had concentrated fiercely upon the levium. That half-legendary deposit of the most mysterious of elements must be found, or all that they had paid in pain and hardship and lives would have been for nothing. If old Thorn Laurel, years ago, had actually come this dreadful way and found the levium, it must still be here.

They reached the truncated summit of the peak, and crouched flat for a few moments lest the ferocious currents that raged at these heights should tear them off the rock. They found themselves clinging to the jagged rim of the crater itself.

"Do we have to go down into that?" Philip Sidney was asking a little dazedly, having raised his head to peer down into the crater.

"Laurel's directions said the levium was *in* this crater," North answered. "He must have found a way down into it."

The crater pit was a roughly vertical shaft more than a hundred feet across, dropping into black, lightless depths. The walls of this volcanic tube, like the slopes of the peak outside, were crusted with ledges and ridges of frozen lava, and red living lava glowed at its bottom.

"I see a way down the northern wall of the pit," Whitey exclaimed. "But it looks risky."

"It must be the way Laurel went down, for it's the only possible one," North said. "Come on."

They went around to the north side of the crater, crouching low against the screaming currents of smoke. Once they had started down into the crater-tube, they escaped the main force of the atmospheric currents. But the shuddering of the crater to each rumbling crash of thunder was more dangerous here.

For this trail down into the interior of the crater was more precarious even than the one outside. They had to grope their way from ledge to ledge, conscious that a slip would mean a tumble into the living lava that glowed redly at the far bottom of the shaft.

Then John North glimpsed a little below them a faint glow of *blue* light from an aperture in the crater wall. His heart bounded.

"I think we've found it," he exclaimed hoarsely. "Come on…"

THEY dropped onto a shelving ledge, from the side of which the aperture opened into the crater's mass. The opening was man-high.

North entered it, passing into a small cavern that was one of the many bubble-like spaces honeycombing the crater. But this little space inside the rock glowed with a weird, frosty blue brilliance. The light came from the roof of the cave. They all three looked upward.

"It's the levium!" Whitey yelled.

"But Johnny, look at the *size* of it—"

Sidney's voice was quivering. "It can't be real. There can't be that much levium anywhere."

North's heart was pounding with excitement that was mingled with a strange feeling of awe as he looked up at that wonder of the fiery moon.

Seemingly suspended just under the vaulted rock roof of the little cave, hung an irregular ovoid of dense, stony matter that glowed from every atom with that pure, frosty blue brilliance. Its mass was almost seven feet along its greatest length, and nearly that wide and thick.

It was like a shining blue sun, hanging there at the cavern roof. But it was not really hanging there, North knew. That stupendous mass of levium was really pressing *upward* against the roof, seeking vainly to escape from this pocket in which it had long been trapped.

North could only guess the geologic history of this levium mass. Caught inside the fiery mass of Oberon when the moon began to solidify, the levium had through the ages pressed upward and upward, seeking to fly off into space with all the peculiar reversed gravitation that it alone possessed, yet trapped here in this cave for perhaps many ages.

"Now we know why Thorn Laurel brought back only a scrap of the levium," North said hoarsely. "No one man could handle this mass."

Sidney reached upward with his steelite bar and chipped a small fragment of the shining levium loose. He grasped it in his hand and pulled it down.

It struggled in the young Company officer's hand, to fall upward. And when he released it, it shot up and smacked against the roof.

"Unbelievable," he muttered, dazedly. "No wonder the stuff is so super-valuable. It alone among the elements can defy gravitation."

"Johnny, how are we going to get the stuff out of here?" Whitey asked tautly. "We can't simply carry it—it would tend to fall upward every minute. We couldn't hold it."

"There's only one possible way to get it out," North sweated. "We'll have to lash it to a mass of ordinary rock heavy enough to counterbalance the levium's minus weight."

They found such a mass of rock in one corner of the little cave—a great chunk that had been shaken from the wall by the continuous rumbling convulsions of Thunder Moon.

Standing upon it, they pried at the hanging levium mass with their steelite bars, seeking to get the cables around it and draw it down. But as they started to haul the levium downward, chunks of rock began falling from the cavern roof against which it had been pressing.

"Johnny, the whole roof may come down on us," Whitey exclaimed.

North realized the peril. The mass of levium, pressing upward for ages, had strained and split the cavern roof. If they removed the levium now, the one support of the roof would be gone, and the continuous quakes of Thunder Moon would soon shake down the whole cave upon them.

"We've got to get the stuff out of here quickly," North declared. "Hurry and lash it to the rock."

IT TOOK the strength of all three of them to haul the levium down from the roof by the cables they had passed around it. As they hastily lashed it to the mass of black rock, more chunks fell from above.

Lashed to the rock, the reversed weight of the levium was more than counterbalanced. The whole bound mass of levium and rock together had only a few pounds of positive weight.

"The next strong quake will bring the whole cave down now," North said warningly. "Hurry and get out of here."

"Not yet..." rasped a familiar, harsh voice.

They spun around. Charles Berdeau's tall, insulite-clad figure stood in the entrance of the cave, with an atom-pistol leveled upon them.

Berdeau came swiftly into the little cavern, and they could glimpse the figure of Kells on the ledge outside. And Berdeau's black eyes were flaring with triumph inside his helmet as he covered the petrified three.

"I still hold a hand in this game," North," the gambler snapped. "You didn't stop to think that your friend Dorak might pass out from pain and give Kells and me a chance to work free, did you?"

North knew that Berdeau was going to kill them and that neither he nor Sidney could get out their own weapons in time to prevent it.

But for just a moment, Berdeau's fingers lingered on the trigger as the gambler glanced exultantly at the incredible, shining mass of levium.

"The treasure of Thunder Moon," he whispered, trembling with avidity. "The biggest pot of all—"

Rumbling reverberation of another shuddering quake shook them at that moment. And from the split roof fell a shower of rocky chunks that smashed down on Berdeau's outstretched arm and pistol and sent the gambler reeling wildly back.

"The whole cave is coming down!" Whitey Jones yelled wildly. "Out of here!"

They grabbed the big bound mass of levium and rock and dragged it furiously toward the entrance of the cave. The unarmed criminal Kells who had been on the ledge outside had fled.

Berdeau had got to his feet, was trying drunkenly to find his atom-gun, as North and Sidney struggled convulsively to drag the levium mass through the narrow opening. But with a crashing roar, the whole roof of the cave gave way and poured down on the gambler in a stony shower.

The archway of the aperture was settling, the opening collapsing upon North and Sidney. But Whitey sprang into that closing opening, his giant form bracing with Herculean effort to hold up the settling rock masses with his great back and shoulders.

It gave North and Sidney the moment in which to thrust the levium-and-rock mass outside, onto the ledge.

But when North turned, Whitey's giant shoulders were buckling under the weight of collapsing rock, and his voice came to them as a gasping groan.

"Johnny—"

North would never forget the love and despair that shone in Whitey's eyes as his great head bowed beneath the crushing weight.

Even as North sprang wildly back to haul the giant clear, he was shaken from his feet by the ultimate crash of collapsing rock as the whole cave crumpled in upon itself.

He staggered up on his knees and there was no more cave or opening, and there was only a great mass of new-fallen rock slabs where Whitey Jones had stood. He beat with clenched fists on the rock, and his voice was strangled.

"Whitey! Whitey!"

But he knew that Whitey was dead and buried, like Berdeau, beneath tons of rock that he had held back for that last moment of their escape.

SIDNEY'S shaking, urgent voice penetrated through North's agony of grief. The young officer was clinging to the levium mass as they crouched on the shuddering ledge of the crater pit wall.

"Kells got away!" Sidney was shouting. "He fled back up the trail—he didn't have any weapon but he'll use our raft to escape if we don't stop him."

North felt dazed and unreal, yet even so he roused himself to action.

"You bring the levium," he said hoarsely to Sidney. "I'll go after him."

He clawed his way back up to the crater-shaft's summit, and every moment of the way there was only one thought ringing in his stunned mind. Whitey was dead—Whitey was dead.

When he came out onto the summit of the crater, North saw Kells' insulite-suited figure scrambling frantically down the slope of the peak. He flung himself fiercely in pursuit, heedless now of all risks.

But Kells, looking fearfully back at him, increased his frenzied speed. The criminal had already reached the ledge on the shore of the Flaming Ocean, and was untying the stone raft there and shoving it convulsively out onto the burning lava flood.

North drew his atom-gun and shot, but Kells dodged fearfully back and escaped the crashing bolt. The stone raft was floating further out onto the flaming sea. Desperately, Kells ran and leaped for it—

He leaped short, in his heavy moon-shoes. North saw the criminal hit the molten lava and heard a ghastly scream mercifully choked off in his spacesuit phone. When he sickly looked again, there was no sign of Kells in the lava flood. The dark stone raft was floating serenely away.

North went back to the summit, and helped Sidney drag the unwieldy mass of levium and stone down to the ledge at the crater's base. Then they bent over Dorak's still form.

Dorak lay still and unconscious, but he was breathing.

"He'll live if we can get him out of here," Sidney said. "But how, North? The raft's gone—"

Dully, North roused himself again. "We may be able to cut another raft from the rock of the crater," he muttered. "But I'm afraid it's too heavy a stone to float."

They made a trial, chipping loose a block of the basic rock of the crater and tossing it into the flaming sea. It sank slowly under the hissing crimson flood.

"I thought so," North said heavily. "We're marooned here. We can't possibly get away, for that's the only kind of rock there is here."

Sidney cried out. "But even if we are finished, what about Aline, and Nova, and Steenie? They're over there in the ship—they won't be able to get away from this moon either. The girls aren't pilots. And if they tried by themselves to make another stone raft and come out for us, the Fieries would surely overwhelm them."

North thought. "They've only got one chance to get away," he said finally. "That's Steenie. If he could pilot the ship off this moon—"

"But he's space-struck," Sidney exclaimed. "North, a man like that can't pilot a ship..."

"He used to be a great pilot, years ago," North muttered. "His mind, dimmed as it is, may remember a little. It's their only chance to get away."

North spent some minutes attaching Sidney's spacesuit phone battery to his own instrument. The redoubled power might enable the short-radius instrument to reach the *Meteor*.

He spoke urgently. "John North calling the *Meteor*."

THERE came no answer. He called, over and over again. "They'll surely think to listen for possible messages when we don't come back," he said desperately.

But it was almost an hour before a wildly excited girl's voice rang suddenly in his ears.

"Sailor, is that you? This is Nova! I was worried and tried turning on the audiophone, and—"

"Nova, listen... We've got the levium but we can't get away from here." North told her rapidly what had happened. "You have got to get away from this moon in the ship, and get to Titania for help. It's the only way you can get us out of this."

"But we can't do that," Nova cried. "You can't live out there for the days it would take for us to go and come back with help."

"Of course we can live here that long," North lied. "We found a cache of supplies here that old Thorn Laurel left—oxygen tanks, food, water and a portable heat-tight shelter. When you come back with help, you'll find us here with the levium."

Nova finally agreed. "If you're sure that's the best way we can help you, sailor, we'll do it. Only—how can we get away to Titania? Neither Aline nor I can pilot a ship."

"I know, but maybe Steenie can," North said. "I want you to let me talk to Steenie."

He waited while Nova went for the space-struck man. And he saw Philip Sidney smiling strangely at him.

"That was a good lie you told, North," Sidney said in a low voice. "If you hadn't told that, they'd never have agreed to leave."

North nodded. "They'll come back with help, if they get safely away. We'll be dead—but the levium will be here, to be used as we planned."

He broke off as he heard the click of the audiophone in the *Meteor* being turned on again. Then came Steenie's doubtful voice.

"Steenie, listen—this is Johnny," North said, speaking slowly and clearly to reach that dimmed mind. "Steenie, you want to pilot the ship, don't you?"

"Yes, Johnny," came the eager answer. "Will you let me pilot it now?"

"Do you think you can, Steenie?" North asked tensely. "It's been years since you were at the controls of any ship, you know. Do you think you remember enough?"

"I think I will remember it all when I get my hands on the space-stick, John."

"Then listen, Steenie," sweated North. "Here's what you must do. You must take the ship straight up away from this moon. You must head for Titania, and land at the spaceport of Moontown."

Steenie's voice came in a puzzled, halting question. "But what about you and the others, Johnny? You're not going to stay on this place, are you? It isn't a good place to stay."

"I know, but we've got to stay here," North explained. "We can't get away from this peak. You have to go for help."

"But I can come out for you in the ship," Steenie proposed eagerly. "I can come and get you and then we'll all go away from here together."

"No, *Steenie!*" North's voice rang urgently. "You mustn't try that. There's no place here where the ship can land."

"But I could make a suspension landing long enough to let you get in the ship," the space-struck pilot declared in his clear, childish voice.

"You mustn't try it, Steenie. The atmospheric currents are hellish here—no pilot could make a suspension-landing here without crashing. You've got to do as I say and take off from this moon—"

NORTH paused but there was no answer. He yelled frantically into the transmitter in his helmet. "Steenie, listen to me. Don't try that or you'll kill yourself and the girls too—"

"North, *look!*" Philip Sidney's stabbing cry made North raise his eyes swiftly.

Out there to the south across the flaming lava sea, something was rising through the smoke. It was the big, long bulk of the *Meteor*, ascending on the fiery blast of its keel tubes.

Its tail tubes jetted and it came rushing out low above the surging molten lava, toward them. Its low altitude and high speed seemed carrying it toward a headlong crash against the crater.

"Steenie, go back!" North screamed vainly into his transmitter.

It was too late. The massive bulk of the battered *Meteor* was rushing down toward the narrow ledge on which they crouched.

Staccato thunder of its roaring rocket-tubes drowned out even the rumbling roar of the quaking moon. The ship was dropping beside them, dropping to destruction in the flaming lava—

Its keel-tubes jetted blinding gush of fire downward, jets that spumed the lava beneath to fiery spray. And, poised precariously upon those flaming columns and lurching and rocking to the wild currents that screamed about them, the ship hovered in the suspension-landing.

"This way, North!" Sidney was yelling wildly.

The airlock door of the hovering ship was but a few feet in front of them. They plunged toward it, dragging the ponderous levium and rock mass and thrusting it into the ship.

It seemed madness to think that any pilot in the universe could hold a suspension-landing, most superhumanly difficult of all piloting feats, for these precious seconds in the screaming smoke currents. But Steenie was holding it there. Playing the keel and lateral tubes like an organ of fire, holding and balancing the ship—

North found himself in the airlock with Sidney and the levium mass. He clawed the outer door shut, tore open the inner door and yelled hoarsely, "Up, Steenie—*up!*"

He was flung headlong as the *Meteor* roared upward through the raging smoke as though flung by a giant catapult. Up and up, out through the swirling smoke and ashes of Thunder Moon, out toward clear space and the friendly stars.

Nova and Aline were beside North, helping him up, sobbing from relief and emotion. But he went past them, he staggered to the control room where Steenie crouched with the space-stick held far back.

Steenie's face was blazing, transfigured, for this brief moment—all the flaming genius of his great past living for these few seconds in his brain once more as he sent the *Meteor* roaring out and out into the void.

And then the ship was droning through clear space under the great, mild green eye of Uranus, and Thunder Moon was a sullen crimson sphere falling astern, and Steenie's face became mild and childlike as always.

He looked anxiously up at North. "Did I do it all right, Johnny?" he asked anxiously. "Did I?"

North's hand was shaking as he laid it on the other's shoulder. "You did what no other pilot in the System could have done, Steenie."

Steenie smiled, the pleased smile of a happy child.

"I was a good pilot, once," he said.

CHAPTER TEN
The Monument

CREAKING in every beam as though tired from its long journey, the *Meteor* sank toward the night side of Earth. Upon the moonlit convexity below, the lights of New York were a brilliant blaze. Around the black blot of the spaceport glowed the friendly red and green beacons.

North brought the ship down slowly. And when it had landed, and the drone of the cycs was replaced by a new silence that seemed very heavy, he sat for a moment motionless in the pilot chair before he unstrapped. Then, shoulders sagging, he went back to the cabin.

Sidney had opened the door, and the men who had been waiting with a stretcher and rocket-car had come in. They were putting Dorak on the stretcher. The spaceman's leg had been treated at Titania, and hospital care would save it for him though he would be crippled for life.

Dorak looked up at North past the others, and his pallid face was queerly intent. "Johnny—"

"We'll talk later, Jan," North said quietly. "You go along with them now and rest. And Steenie, I want you to go too—to help take care of Jan."

Steenie brightened. "I'll take care of him. But you'll come later, Johnny?"

"I'll come later."

They went out, and Aline's fine eyes dimmed as she looked after them. Her voice was husky as she turned to North.

"They, and all the other old spacemen like them—they'll never want for anything again," she said huskily. "Half the levium goes to them as we planned. And it isn't enough."

Sidney told North earnestly, "I didn't have a chance to talk to you on the way in, North. But I wanted to tell you—there'll be no trouble with the Company. I'm resigning there, and I'll testify that Aline had actually bought this ship. They'll have no case at all."

North nodded his thanks. "What about the levium? Have you made any arrangements?"

Aline nodded eagerly. "Philip sent a message from Titania. Men will be here to take the levium to safekeeping. I think they're here now."

It was indeed the armed guards and armored rocket-truck that had come for the treasure. With curious lack of emotion, North watched them load it into the truck.

Sidney came back to him as he stood there in the moonlight outside the ship. The young officer's clean-cut face was uncertain.

"North, there's something else I didn't have a chance to tell you. Aline and I—"

North smiled faintly and nodded. "I know, Sidney. It was clear enough all the way back that you two love each other."

Sidney seemed distressed. "I guess I was afraid to tell you. I thought maybe you and Aline—maybe you—"

North shook his head tiredly. "It wasn't ever like that, Sidney. Aline is fine and dear, and she gave us the chance to go to space again and do something for our old comrades. And I think she's fond of me as one of her father's old friends. But that's all there ever was to it."

Sidney's face showed his earnest relief, as he turned. Aline and Nova Smith had come up.

The small blonde star-girl held out her hand to North. Her voice was light. "Goodbye, sailor—and thanks for the lift back to Earth."

"Why, Nova, we all ought to be thanking you," North told her. "If it hadn't been for you—"

"Oh, forget it," she replied with a shrug. "A star-girl's always running into trouble. I was just trying to get out of it myself."

She turned almost brusquely away before North could say more. Aline was speaking eagerly. "Philip and I—all of us—we're going to go together. Come on."

BUT John North hung back. "You go on ahead. There's something I've got to do here—about the ship—"

Doubtfully, they turned away. And North was left standing alone in the moonlight by the battered side of the silent *Meteor*.

He started walking slowly across the spaceport, toward the soaring moonlit shaft of the Monument to the Space Pioneers. A strong wind was blowing gustily through the night, and it brought him the sounds of a Venus liner being readied for takeoff, and the music and laughing voices of the passengers holding bon voyage celebration in the nearby Spaceport Cafe.

But North only half heard these things as he walked with dragging steps toward the monument. He did not know why he had come here, as he stood looking up at the soaring shaft. He felt only a dim ache somehow to feel less alone.

He remembered the day they had landed here on their return with Carew from the second voyage. He remembered the cheering crowds, the bright sunlight, Mike Connor grinning and joking, Whitey's tall young figure over them all—

North bent forward and tried to read the names lettered in bronze on the pedestal, the names of those who had sailed with Johnson and Carew and Wenzi. His own name was there but he was not seeking that. He was looking beneath the immortal names of the great leaders, and name after name in those lists brought phantoms to stand beside him in the windy night.

Jason Peters...

"—ain't nobody goin' to keep me from goin' to space again once more."

Michael Connor...

"—always wanted to die this way, holding a pretty girl and a bottle."

Harley Steen...

"I was a good pilot, wasn't I?"

Whiteman Jones...

"Johnny—"

He could read no more. His throat was an aching tightness, and something blurred his eyes. They were singing now over in the Spaceport Cafe but the sound seemed to come from a great distance.

A small hand grasped his sleeve.

"Sailor..."

He looked down at Nova's face, white and strained in the moonlight.

"Sailor, I *couldn't* leave you—I knew you'd be coming here," she was saying huskily.

THE wind brought the distant song clear to their ears. It was the old song that had lived on to become the popular refrain of these days of otherworld travel.

"We'll build a stairway to the stars—"

North gestured toward the gleaming names upon the pedestal, and his voice was choking.

"They built a stairway to the stars, Nova. And now they're gone—they're gone and forgotten—"

"Sailor, don't." Nova was crying, clinging to him. "I know how you feel, but you're not alone. You'll always have me, sailor, if you want me—if you just want me—"

"Why, Nova—." He looked down at her tear-stained face, wonderingly. "I know I'm only a star-girl—," she began.

"You're the bravest, finest girl I ever met," he told her. "Any man would want you. But I'm old—"

She buried her head against his shoulder, without replying. And North felt strange warmth melt that frozen tightness in his chest.

He held her so, in the moonlight. Held her, while the Venus liner rose with ponderous thunder of rockets, streaking a towering column of fire toward the zenith, dwarfing the stone shaft beside him by the fiery splendor of its greater and more enduring monument.

THE END

If you've enjoyed this book, you will not want to miss these terrific titles…

ARMCHAIR SCI-FI, FANTASY, & HORROR DOUBLE NOVELS, $12.95 each

D-1 **THE GALAXY RAIDERS** by William P. McGivern
SPACE STATION #1 by Frank Belknap Long

D-2 **THE PROGRAMMED PEOPLE** by Jack Sharkey
SLAVES OF THE CRYSTAL BRAIN by William Carter Sawtelle

D-3 **YOU'RE ALL ALONE** by Fritz Leiber
THE LIQUID MAN by Bernard C. Gilford

D-4 **CITADEL OF THE STAR LORDS** by Edmund Hamilton
VOYAGE TO ETERNITY by Milton Lesser

D-5 **IRON MEN OF VENUS** by Don Wilcox
THE MAN WITH ABSOLUTE MOTION by Noel Loomis

D-6 **WHO SOWS THE WIND...** by Rog Phillips
THE PUZZLE PLANET by Robert A. W. Lowndes

D-7 **PLANET OF DREAD** by Murray Leinster
TWICE UPON A TIME by Charles L. Fontenay

D-8 **THE TERROR OUT OF SPACE** by Dwight V. Swain
QUEST OF THE GOLDEN APE by Ivar Jorgensen and Adam Chase

D-9 **SECRET OF MARRACOTT DEEP** by Henry Slesar
PAWN OF THE BLACK FLEET by Mark Clifton.

D-10 **BEYOND THE RINGS OF SATURN** by Robert Moore Williams
A MAN OBSESSED by Alan E. Nourse

ARMCHAIR SCIENCE FICTION CLASSICS, $12.95 each

C-1 **THE GREEN MAN**
by Harold M. Sherman

C-2 **A TRACE OF MEMORY**
By Keith Laumer

C-3 **INTO PLUTONIAN DEPTHS**
by Stanton A. Coblentz

ARMCHAIR MASTERS OF SCIENCE FICTION SERIES, $16.95 each

M-1 **MASTERS OF SCIENCE FICTION, Vol. One**
Bryce Walton—"Dark of the Moon" and other tales

M-2 **MASTERS OF SCIENCE FICTION, Vol. Two**
Jerome Bixby—"One Way Street" and other tales

If you've enjoyed this book, you will not want to miss these terrific titles…

ARMCHAIR SCI-FI & HORROR DOUBLE NOVELS, $12.95 each

D-11 **PERIL OF THE STARMEN** by Kris Neville
THE STRANGE INVASION by Murray Leinster

D-12 **THE STAR LORD** by Boyd Ellanby
CAPTIVES OF THE FLAME by Samuel R. Delany

D-13 **MEN OF THE MORNING STAR** by Edmund Hamilton
PLANET FOR PLUNDER by Hal Clement and Sam Merwin, Jr.

D-14 **ICE CITY OF THE GORGON** by Chester S. Geier and Richard Shaver
WHEN THE WORLD TOTTERED by Lester del Rey

D-15 **WORLDS WITHOUT END** by Clifford D. Simak
THE LAVENDER VINE OF DEATH by Don Wilcox

D-16 **SHADOW ON THE MOON** by Joe Gibson
ARMAGEDDON EARTH by Geoff St. Reynard

D-17 **THE GIRL WHO LOVED DEATH** by Paul W. Fairman
SLAVE PLANET by Laurence M. Janifer

D-18 **SECOND CHANCE** by J. F. Bone
MISSION TO A DISTANT STAR by Frank Belknap Long

D-19 **THE SYNDIC** by C. M. Kornbluth
FLIGHT TO FOREVER by Poul Anderson

D-20 **SOMEWHERE I'LL FIND YOU** by Milton Lesser
THE TIME ARMADA by Fox B. Holden

ARMCHAIR SCIENCE FICTION CLASSICS, $12.95 each

C-4 **CORPUS EARTHLING**
by Louis Charbonneau

C-5 **THE TIME DISSOLVER**
by Jerry Sohl

C-6 **WEST OF THE SUN**
by Edgar Pangborn

ARMCHAIR SCIENCE FICTION & HORROR GEMS SERIES, $12.95 each

G-1 **SCIENCE FICTION GEMS, Vol. One**
Isaac Asimov and others

G-2 **HORROR GEMS, Vol. One**
Carl Jacobi and others

If you've enjoyed this book, you will not want to miss these terrific titles…

ARMCHAIR SCI-FI & HORROR DOUBLE NOVELS, $12.95 each

D-61   **THE MAN WHO STOPPED AT NOTHING** by Paul W. Fairman
            TEN FROM INFINITY by Ivar Jorgensen

D-62   **WORLDS WITHIN** by Rog Phillips
            THE SLAVE by C.M. Kornbluth

D-63   **SECRET OF THE BLACK PLANET** by Milton Lesser
            THE OUTCASTS OF SOLAR III by Emmett McDowell

D-64   **WEB OF THE WORLDS** by Harry Harrison and Katherine MacLean
            RULE GOLDEN by Damon Knight

D-65   **TEN TO THE STARS** by Raymond Z. Gallun
            THE CONQUERORS by David H. Keller, M. D.

D-66   **THE HORDE FROM INFINITY** by Dwight V. Swain
            THE DAY THE EARTH FROZE by Gerald Hatch

D-67   **THE WAR OF THE WORLDS** by H. G. Wells
            THE TIME MACHINE by H. G. Wells

D-68   **STARCOMBERS** by Edmond Hamilton
            THE YEAR WHEN STARDUST FELL by Raymond F. Jones

D-69   **HOCUS-POCUS UNIVERSE** by Jack Williamson
            QUEEN OF THE PANTHER WORLD by Berkeley Livingston

D-70   **BATTERING RAMS OF SPACE** by Don Wilcox
            DOOMSDAY WING by George H. Smith

ARMCHAIR SCIENCE FICTION & FANTASY CLASSICS, $12.95 each

C-19   **EMPIRE OF JEGGA**
            by David V. Reed

C-20   **THE TOMORROW PEOPLE**
            by Judith Merril

C-21   **THE MAN FROM YESTERDAY**
            by Howard Browne as by Lee Francis

C-22   **THE TIME TRADERS**
            by Andre Norton

C-23   **ISLANDS OF SPACE**
            by John W. Campbell

C-24   **THE GALAXY PRIMES**
            by E. E. "Doc" Smith

If you've enjoyed this book, you will not want to miss these terrific titles…

ARMCHAIR SCI-FI & HORROR DOUBLE NOVELS, $12.95 each

D-71   **THE DEEP END** by Gregory Luce
   TO WATCH BY NIGHT by Robert Moore Williams

D-72   **SWORDSMAN OF LOST TERRA** by Poul Anderson
   PLANET OF GHOSTS by David V. Reed

D-73   **MOON OF BATTLE** by J. J. Allerton
   THE MUTANT WEAPON by Murray Leinster

D-74   **OLD SPACEMEN NEVER DIE!** John Jakes
   RETURN TO EARTH by Bryan Berry

D-75   **THE THING FROM UNDERNEATH** by Milton Lesser
   OPERATION INTERSTELLAR by George O. Smith

D-76   **THE BURNING WORLD** by Algis Budrys
   FOREVER IS TOO LONG by Chester S. Geier

D-77   **THE COSMIC JUNKMAN** by Rog Phillips
   THE ULTIMATE WEAPON by John W. Campbell

D-78   **THE TIES OF EARTH** by James H. Schmitz
   CUE FOR QUIET by Thomas L. Sherred

D-79   **SECRET OF THE MARTIANS** by Paul W. Fairman
   THE VARIABLE MAN by Philip K. Dick

D-80   **THE GREEN GIRL** by Jack Williamson
   THE ROBOT PERIL by Don Wilcox

ARMCHAIR SCIENCE FICTION CLASSICS, $12.95 each

C-25   **THE STAR KINGS**
 b   y Edmond Hamilton

C-26   **NOT IN SOLITUDE**
   by Kenneth Gantz

C-32   **PROMETHEUS II**
   by S. J. Byrne

ARMCHAIR SCIENCE FICTION & HORROR GEMS SERIES, $12.95 each

G-7   **SCIENCE FICTION GEMS, Vol. Seven**
   Jack Sharkey and others

G-8   **HORROR GEMS, Vol. Eight**
   Seabury Quinn and others

If you've enjoyed this book, you will not want to miss these terrific titles…

ARMCHAIR SCI-FI, FANTASY, & HORROR DOUBLE NOVELS, $12.95 each

D-81   **THE LAST PLEA** by Robert Bloch
THE STATUS CIVILIZATION by Robert Sheckley

D-82   **WOMAN FROM ANOTHER PLANET** by Frank Belknap Long
HOMECALLING by Judith Merril

D-83   **WHEN TWO WORLDS MEET** by Robert Moore Williams
THE MAN WHO HAD NO BRAINS by Jeff Sutton

D-84   **THE SPECTRE OF SUICIDE SWAMP** by E. K. Jarvis
IT'S MAGIC, YOU DOPE! by Jack Sharkey

D-85   **THE STARSHIP FROM SIRIUS** by Rog Phillips
FINAL WEAPON by Everett Cole

D-86   **TREASURE ON THUNDER MOON** by Edmond Hamilton
TRAIL OF THE ASTROGAR by Henry Haase

D-87   **THE VENUS ENIGMA** by Joe Gibson
THE WOMAN IN SKIN 13 by Paul W. Fairman

D-88   **THE MAD ROBOT** by William P. McGivern
THE RUNNING MAN by J. Holly Hunter

D-89   **VENGEANCE OF KYVOR** by Randall Garrett
AT THE EARTH'S CORE by Edgar Rice Burroughs

D-90   **DWELLERS OF THE DEEP** by Don Wilcox
NIGHT OF THE LONG KNIVES by Fritz Leiber

ARMCHAIR SCIENCE FICTION CLASSICS, $12.95 each

C-28   **THE MAN FROM TOMORROW**
by Stanton A. Cobllentz

C-29   **THE GREEN MAN OF GRAYPEC**
by Festus Pragnell

C-30   **THE SHAVER MYSTERY, Book Four**
by Richard S. Shaver

ARMCHAIR MASTERS OF SCIENCE FICTION SERIES, $16.95 each

MS-7   **MASTERS OF SCIENCE FICTION AND FANTASY, Vol. Seven**
Lester del Rey, "The Band Played On" and other tales

MS-8   **MASTERS OF SCIENCE FICTION, Vol. Eight**
Milton Lesser, "'A' is for Android" and other tales

TERROR FROM DEEP SPACE...

The freighter Astrogar *had disappeared somewhere in the void, seemingly without a trace. Then she was found free-floating in deep space, terribly damaged, but not as damaged as the mind of the spaceman who was found inside her.*

He tried to tell of a dreadful, impending menace…one that could possibly destroy whole worlds! No one believed him except his daughter. She went to the dregs of the space planes to find the answers she sought and to prove her father was more than a raving madman. She soon found Curt Vaughn, and with him a giant Venusian. Together they set out to solve a deep space mystery—the solution to which might hold dire consequences for the entire Solar System…

CAST OF CHARACTERS

CURT VAUGHN
This news hunting space correspondent was looking for the story of a lifetime—and found it on an uncharted asteroid.

DUEELA
This Ganymedian girl had secrets—one of them was in a missing spaceship, but could she trust a space reporter to help her?

KOERBER
Ruthless, rich, and powerful, he would spare no expense and stop at nothing to get at the secrets of the Astrogar.

KRAAZ
He was Koerber's lackey assigned to keep tabs on Vaughn and let him know when they hit pay dirt.

THE SILASTAH
This creature was the creation of many scientists and had the mental powers of all of the best scientific minds of his world.

TARNUFF
Big—and ugly—this cunning space-trading Martian was always ready to take a life for money.

TRAIL OF THE THE ASTROGAR

By
HENRY HASSE

ARMCHAIR FICTION
PO Box 4369, Medford, Oregon   97501-0168

CHAPTER ONE

CURT VAUGHN faced the big Ganymedian. His gray eyes swept across the man's stolid features, clashed with the chill stare. All hope went out of Curt. No compromising here. He knew these people, knew that further argument would be futile. May as well get it over with.

Curt moistened his lips. With a shrug of resignation he slid his precious electro-camera across the counter.

"Okay then, make it sixty credits. Earth, Mars, or Ganymede, you guys are all alike."

He pocketed the reclaim stub that the Ganymedian loan broker handed him, and the sixty Interplanet Credits.

"I'll be claiming that camera again in a few days. It'd better be here."

Curt went into the murky street of Ganymede City, pulled the collar of his space tunic up against the night chill. Jupiter lay across the horizon like a great gloating nemesis.

"So it's come to this again." Curt muttered grimly as he strode along. "Why in the name of the Great Red Spot do I continue in this News-Service game, anyway? Gannett—if he doesn't come through with my remittance..."

For the hundredth time Curt Vaughn wondered what could have gone wrong. He was a free-lance correspondent and a good one, selling scoop stories to the highest bidder, which was usually Gannett of Earth News Bureau. Following a hot lead, Curt had gotten out of Europa in time to witness the uprising of the savage outlanders against the Colonists. The Tri-Planet Patrol had squelched the uprising after a week of bloody fighting; but Curt had obtained the story despite censorship, and some marvelous pictures as well. He'd barely escaped with them and his life.

Crossing to Ganymede, he'd sent the story and pictures through the outlaw Tele-Magnum Station. They reached Earth, too, for he'd received the "okay" reply. Gannett had promised a handsome bonus on a scoop like this. Then where was his remittance? It should have arrived at Interplanet Bank here at Ganymede City three days ago.

Was the man who signed the checks at Earth Office "away on vacation?" Curt laughed mirthlessly. He'd heard that one before, too.

Curt Vaughn came suddenly alert now. His straying thoughts centered again, with that supernal sense of keening he'd learned through endless adventures in the spaceways. He had glimpsed no figure behind him in the abysmal gloom. He had heard no sound of footsteps. But with unerring instinct, Curt Vaughn knew he was being followed.

HE DIDN'T pause in his stride; he didn't look back. Somehow his steps had led him into one of the dark narrow streets bordering the spaceport. Now he glimpsed a dull greenish glow ahead, which could only be one of the sub-level saloons.

Curt reached there and took the stairs downward—but only a few steps, then he crouched back into the shadows and waited, staring up to the street level.

His pursuer soon appeared. The man stood limned for a moment in the overhead light. Curt let his breath out slowly, then frowned a little.

"Just as I thought—the Jovian again. Same one. I'm sure of it. He's a persistent cuss." Curt had been aware of this man all afternoon, seemed to encounter him wherever he went. Now Curt eased the ato-blast in his belt and remounted the stairs, determined to end the matter once and for all.

The Jovian watched him come. He grinned broadly, almost child-like. The grin didn't fool Curt. All Jovians grinned. Some of them grinned while breaking a man's vertebrae. This was one of the big ones, Curt noticed, over seven feet tall with bulk to match. And he was ugly, with long reaching arms and wiry hair and a face that looked as if he'd slept in it.

Curt came fairly close, raised a hand in greeting. "Heigh! Something I can do for you?"

No answer. But even in this dim light Curt could see a flash of intelligence in the heavy-lidded amber eyes.

"Now look, friend, I want no trouble but I want some answers. You followed me from my hotel this evening. You followed me to the Interplanet Bank. Then to the spaceport. And then here. It gets kind of annoying." Curt balanced on his toes, kept his hand near his ato-blast. "Spill! I know you understand English, most of you do—"

The Jovian eased forward. Curt leaped aside and the gun was in his hand, but only for a second. He hadn't expected such speed from such a bulk. A hand shot out, powerful fingers clamped around Curt's gun-wrist. The weapon clattered to the pavement. Curt lashed out with his left fist, felt it crash against the bone of the Jovian's jaw. Then…both of his wrists were clamped and helpless.

The Jovian still grinned.

"Kraaz unnerstand Earth talk—yez. You come 'long with me now, not?"

Curt struggled. His toes almost left the ground, as the grip tightened. Nerves along both arms shrieked in agony. He tried to bring up a knee, but Kraaz shoved him hard against the building, bearing down with his weight. The breath came out of Curt with a quick *whoosh*.

"You come 'long peazeful, not?"

"I come along peaceful yes." Curt gasped. "Just let go of me, you grinning ape!"

Kraaz nodded. He shoved the Earthman away, then retrieved the ato-blast, thrust it into his pocket. He motioned Curt to precede him down the stairs, to the saloon.

"You will remember pleaze, I have the gun."

"Sure. But you do all right without one," Curt rubbed his aching wrists.

Kraaz walked beside him as they pushed through the doors. Curt knew this place. It was rendezvous for the cutthroat scum of all planets, and named sardonically enough, the *Green Halo*. Through a haze of smoke he saw the motley little groups at the tables and bar. There were leathery, heavy-lidded Martians, eternally sullen and suspicious. A scattering of frail Venusians, pallid and dreamy-eyed and deceptively docile, lips purplish from chewing the dreadful *eishn* stems which Earthmen shunned. A few Earthmen were there too, from the recently arrived freighters; they retained that swaggering superiority which made them the most hated men in the system.

CURT'S mind was racing now, as they threaded their way through the place. Where was Kraaz taking him? More important, who had sent Kraaz after him, and why? Then Curt remembered something. These Jovians, for all their strength, became truly docile with a few drinks under their belt. Yes, and they became voluble.

Curt took a chance, headed for the bar. "I'll buy the drinks, Kraaz."

"No. No drinkz." Kraaz gripped him fiercely by the arm, and Curt felt steel in those fingers. "We go thiz way." He was steering Curt toward a door at the end of the room.

This Jovian was no fool, Curt mused. He had been instructed well.

As they neared the end of the bar, a figure half turned from the throng pressing there. It was a girl, a swarthy-faced Ganymedian, one of the typical *habitués* of these places. She staggered into Curt. Part of her drink slopped across his tunic. She mouthed a guttural apology—but in the same instant, her hand found his, and Curt felt a folded piece of paper pressed into his palm.

Kraaz hadn't noticed. They passed through the far door, and Curt took the opportunity to slip the paper into his pocket. They went along a low-ceilinged passage, then into another room, little more than a cubicle, quite bare of furnishings. Kraaz pressed a stud in the wall. Light swam across a section of it, making it a visi-screen. The leering face of a Ganymedian appeared there. He seemed to recognize Kraaz, and nodded. A moment later, an entire wall of the room slid silently downward, revealing a stone stairway.

They headed down into stygian darkness. Curt felt his stomach rebel at a blast of unclean air. He stumbled along beside the huge-striding Jovian. Now, he had time to think of the native girl and the folded note. For just an instant, Curt had glimpsed her eyes, and they had been crystal clear with a peculiar hint of pleading. But Curt shrugged now. He had troubles of his own.

He tugged against his captor's grip. "Slow down a little, Kraaz. Where you taking me?"

"The bozz wantz to talk with you."

"The boss, eh. And who's the boss?"

"Zoon now you will zee." Even in this pitchy blackness Curt felt that the Jovian was still grinning.

THE stairs leveled off into what seemed to bean endless network of ill-lighted streets. Curt didn't need to ask questions now. He knew where he was. In the subterranean section of Ganymede City, of which he'd heard so much. It was rumored that the recent, organized piracy of the spaceways stemmed from here, under leadership of an individual who remained nameless and never left the place.

It was not known whether this man was Earthian, Martian or Ganymedian. The Tri-Planet Patrol had sought him out for the past several years. Curt recalled stories of Patrolmen having entered this sub-city in cunning disguise. They had never been known to come out again.

"What a scoop this would be!" Curt thought as he kept pace with Kraaz in the encompassing gloom. And he felt a pang of regret for having parted with his camera, which was equipped with infrared and would have recorded their route.

Kraaz knew the way perfectly. For an hour they traversed endless passages and cross streets. Several times Curt had glimpses of lighted underground buildings, and the sound of men at work reached his ears. Clang of metal on metal. The ascending hiss of atomic furnaces. Repair shops, Curt thought. Whoever this pirate was, he was well equipped.

"Almozt now, we are there," Kraaz said at last.

Light appeared far ahead. It came from a low-structured but pretentious building. They entered, and it was as though they had emerged from a darksome hell into a cleaner, brighter world. The air here was fresh. Subdued and soothing lights flanked the paneled walls. Along the floor of the entrance hall lay a rug, which Curt recognized as Venusian *kalado* fur, expensive enough to ransom a world.

They came to a wide door at the end of the hall. Kraaz knocked softly. There was a long wait, during which Curt had an uncanny feeling that they were being examined through some hidden device. Then the door swung silently open.

Curt had a confused impression of brilliant lighting and indiscriminate luxury. Magnificent, ceiling-high tapestries covered the walls. Priceless ornaments from every planet were here in profuse disarray. Some were museum pieces, such as the desk of extinct Martian *jragua* wood at the end of the room.

Then Curt was beyond all amazement as his gaze centered on the face of the man behind this desk. A large man, vigorous and dominant, with a striking shock of white in the middle of his dark bushy hair. A man whose eyes were black and depthless as the outer reaches of space. But one didn't notice these things. What one noticed, was the horrible burn that lay livid across one entire side of his face; an eyelid pulled grotesquely down into a perpetual leer; the withered and useless arm lying across the desk.

Curt noticed these things, then let his breath out very slowly. For he felt he knew this man, or had once known him. Once, yes, long ago, when the man had not been like this. And Curt's brain churned, trying to bring back the remembrance.

Meanwhile the man was speaking softly.

"You have done well, Kraaz, thank you. You may leave us now." He waited until the door had closed behind the Jovian, then turned piercing black eyes upon Curt. "And you, Curt Vaughn, come forward. Come, have a chair and talk with me. It has been a long time."

CHAPTER TWO

CURT leaned back in his chair, inhaled deeply from a cigarette. His cool gray eyes never left the face of the man across the desk. This man smiled a bit sardonically.

"So you remember me, Vaughn. But not like this— eh?"

"Koerber," Curt breathed. "Yes, it's been a long time, eight or nine years—"

"It seems much longer. I often yearn for those days again, Vaughn, when we were freebooting it in the outer planets. I lost track of you right after we made the iridium strike on Titan. What happened?"

"I knew it couldn't last," Curt shrugged. "Earth Corporations getting too strong and greedy, backed up by the Tri-Planet Patrol. I got out just in time."

"You were smart. Lots of the others gave it up too. Only Lohss and Delavan stuck with me. We tried for a claim on Io…"

Curt was trying to avoid looking at this man. Koerber noticed it, smiled grimly and went on:

"Yes, Io. That was to be our last try. By then, the Patrol wasn't fooling with freebooters—they meant business. We had a running battle with them near Io. They brought us down. We crashed in the Ionian crags, and Lohss and Delavan were killed. You see what happened to me." Koerber paused, smiled twistedly. "Strange, the

Patrol being there. Almost as if someone had informed them on us. It could have been one of the others, or—it could have been you."

Curt uncoiled his length slowly from the chair. His words came like icy javelins. "You think that, Koerber? You think I informed?"

Koerber waved him down. "Calm yourself. No, I don't think so, Vaughn, but I'm glad to see you're the same man I used to know. I brought you here for quite another reason." He glanced about at the magnificent appointments of the room. "I haven't done badly, eh Vaughn? And I've given the Patrol plenty to worry about."

"'Suppose you state your business, Koerber."

"Sure. Vaughn, I've been following this News career of yours. It takes you into some pretty tight places. That is good. You prefer to work alone, and that is good, too. Vaughn...I have a job mapped out for you."

"What makes you think I'll work for you, Koerber? I'm through with all that."

"I could state several reasons why you'll work for me," Koerber purred, "but one will be sufficient. This job, if you see it through, will give you as big a News scoop as you've ever had. It's within the law, if that's what's worrying you; just barely within, but that's the way you've been working."

Curt had to grin. "Seems you know a lot about me."

"No man comes, or goes in Ganymede City that I don't know about." Koerber leaned forward. "This job, now. Vaughn, have you ever heard of a man named Landreth?"

THE name seemed familiar. Curt's mind went back across the years—and suddenly he remembered. "You mean Anton Landreth, the man who used to work the asteroid swarms? Sure. I always admired him. Plenty dangerous, those uncharted swarms." Curt came suddenly erect. "Say, don't tell me those crazy stories are cropping up again?"

"That's the man. As for the stories, yes, they still persist—and they may not be as crazy as they sound. Spacemen have heard them in every dive from Mercury to Ganymede, and Landreth became a laughing stock. True, he was a little unbalanced, after his last return from the asteroids. But Vaughn...I'm sure he did find something out there. Something fabulous and wonderful."

Curt shook his head. "But those wild tales! Why, even the Earth authorities wouldn't—"

Koerber motioned Curt to silence, then reached across his desk and pressed a button. A moment later a servant-girl entered—small, dark skinned, Ganymedian. She brought a tray with two glasses and a decanter of *thassium*. Curt was fascinated by the sparkling blue liquor, now forbidden on all the planets, but at the same time he was aware of the girl watching him covertly.

He glanced at her. With an effort, he suppressed a start of surprise. This was the same girl who had slipped the note to him in the saloon. Curt was sure of it a moment later as she leaned forward to pour his drink, and he caught that same urgent look in her eyes.

Koerber hadn't noticed. To hide his emotions, Curt raised the glass to his lips. *What was this girl trying to tell him? Was that look in her eyes a pleading—or a warning?*

"Thank you, Dueela," Koerber was saying. "That will be all."

Curt didn't look at her again. He sipped appreciatively at his drink. Dueela left the room as silently as she'd come.

"AS FOR those wild tales of Landreth's," Koerber went on, "you'll remember they always seemed to take on a peculiar incoherence when he was questioned too closely. As if he was *remembering*—remembering more than his mind could bear. It's no wonder he became a laughing stock."

"He told the Earth authorities of a menace," Curt said very slowly. "A terrible threat on one of the asteroids…something that would *one day* strike at Earth and perhaps the other planets."

"And that's been ten years ago," Koerber reminded. "No, I can't swallow that. But, Vaughn…he found *something* out there, because he was always wanting to get back. He may have been half crazed, but he was clear on that point."

"He wanted to get back? How do you know that?"

"I thought you knew the story. His ship was smashed among those uncharted rocks, but he was lucky enough to blast out toward one of the space lanes. A Patroller found him, half dead from hunger and delirium. They towed his ship back to Earth. I understand he was in a mental institution there for a couple of years. After that he began searching, always searching for his ship—it was named *Astrogar,* I believe. That's how he became a wanderer on every planet, carrying his wild tales with him."

"Searching for the *Astrogar,*" Curt mused. "Certainly a spaceship doesn't vanish in ten years' time. It may change hands. It would probably change name and even design—but it doesn't vanish."

"Exactly." Koerber's black eyes glittered now. "That's why I brought you in on this. I have the money to conduct the search. You still have the youth and capabilities for adventure, besides that unerring news sense. Vaughn...*I want the Astrogar!*"

"And you want it badly. What's in it for me?"

"Half of whatever we realize, plus the news story of course."

Curt hesitated despite the latter inducement. This man Koerber was like a madman pursuing a dream. Was it a dream of riches? But he had riches. A dream of power? But he had power, after a measure. No, it went deeper than that.

"Koerber, I'll see this thing through with you on one condition. You've got to tell me more. Why do you want Landreth's ship *now?* Why now, at this late date? For that matter why was Landreth always searching for it?"

"A little thought would show you why. *Landreth hid something aboard the Astrogar—hid it well.* I believe it to be some sort of data, perhaps a chart giving the exact location of his strange asteroid. Vaughn...just recently Landreth died, and I spoke to him before he died. I learned just that much. There was something aboard the *Astrogar* that he wanted."

Curt's eyes narrowed. "You learned nothing more?"

"Well, there was one more thing." Koerber hesitated. "A name—a strange name that Landreth kept repeating. *The Silastah.* He spoke it with a kind of fear and reverence. Mean anything to you?"

"*Silastah,*" Curt repeated, a dawning of wonderment in his eyes. "That's not from any language I ever heard."

"And it's just as strange to me." Koerber became briskly business-like, took up a pen and wrote a check that he handed to Curt. Curt looked at the amount and whistled.

"No telling where your search will take you. That's enough to cover all expenses, plus a good purchase price for the *Astrogar* when you do find it. I want that ship legally." Koerber's lips twisted down. "And Vaughn, don't get too curious, or too ambitious. You know your job now. See that you do it."

CURT rose. "You know, I *am* getting curious now. Suppose when I find the *Astrogar*, I—"

"You'll bring the *Astrogar* back *here*. I know what's in your mind, Vaughn, so I've taken precautions." Koerber pressed a button. Kraaz strode into the room. "See what I mean? You've met Kraaz, of course. You're going to know him much better, because from now on he'll accompany you wherever you go."

We'll see about that, Curt thought grimly. But he forced a smile, clapped a friendly hand on Kraaz' shoulder.

"Okay, pal. Let's go."

He went out the door with the big hulk of the Jovian right behind him.

CHAPTER THREE

"WHERE firzt?" Kraaz asked with a sidelong grin, as they found themselves once more in the dim streets of the sub-city.

"Back to the *Green Halo,* I guess. Just so we get out of this place." With sudden inspiration Curt added: "I guess you'll have that drink with me now?"

"You guezz wrong. For you all right. No drinkz for me."

Curt shrugged. It was all right; he had plenty of time. He'd get rid of Kraaz sooner or later. For a while they walked in silence through the dim, close-walled streets.

"I can't get to the Bank until tomorrow," Curt mused aloud. "We'll have dinner somewhere, Kraaz, then go back to my hotel. I'll get a room for you."

"Not nezezzary. Zame room iz all right. I ztay with you."

Curt stared at the bulk moving a little ahead of him. It was dawning on him that here was one of those oddities, a Jovian with rare insight and intelligence. Maybe this would be a tougher job than he had supposed.

Kraaz paused in his stride just then and glanced back. He waited for Curt to reach him. But still he stood there, staring into the dimness, holding his head a little sideways as though listening. Then he went striding on. Faster now. Curt hurried to keep pace.

Again the Jovian paused. Curt could just glimpse the white blob of his face. It seemed puzzled.

"What's the matter? Don't tell me you're lost—"

"Quiet! Lizzen."

Curt listened. He heard nothing. Kraaz tugged at his arm, drew him back into a stone archway. Then Curt heard it—footsteps, soft and swift, coming their way. A brush of clothes against the smooth stone wall. Hurried breathing.

A gun was in the Jovian's hand now. Curt realized it must be his own ato-gun. They waited. They could see the vague shadow now, moving along close to the wall.

"Only one," Kraaz murmured. "Wait here." Before Curt realized his intention, Kraaz had stepped down from the archway. He uttered a challenge.

Things happened with incredible swiftness.

A beam of light lashed out and limned the scene. It wasn't the ato-blast. Those beams were white, and this was blue and blinding. It touched Kraaz, sent him staggering back. The beam leaped upward and clung for a terrible moment against his neck. Kraaz crumpled. The ato-gun clattered away from his nerveless fingers.

Curt leaped forward, clawing for the ato-gun. Then he hit the pavement, rolled away into darkness. He was blinded. He heard rather than saw the rush of a dark figure toward him…tried desperately to swing his gun around. Too late. Again the blue beam came. It brushed his neck and clung there.

No pain. Only a vast terrible nervelessness. A giddy feeling as if he were sinking beneath the waters of a dark sea. Then the sea engulfed him.

HOW long had it been? He was swimming upward again, sputtering, fighting against the water. This was very real. Curt opened his eyes. He was lying on something hard. Water dripped from his face and neck.

Then he stared at the figure standing over him. A girl— dark-skinned, angry, Ganymedian. *The* Ganymedian girl! She was about to throw more water on him. Curt managed to pull himself erect and stand swaying against a table. He looked at her again. Yes, she was angry.

Curt grinned, lifted a hand in greeting. "Heigh! I remember you. Name's Dueela, isn't it?" He glanced about him. He was in a room somewhere. This girl's room, obviously.

He faced her again and his eyes went wide. Now she was holding a gun on him, a deadly looking weapon of a type Curt had never seen before.

"So it was *you!* You who blasted me—"

"Yes. I blasted you, and if you don't—"

Curt took a swift, sideward step. His hand came down hard and accurate on her wrist. He twisted, and she cried out. Her fingers loosened. Then Curt had the gun.

"That's better. I feel more like talking now."

"You!" She was furious. "And you call yourself an Earthman!"

"Now what do you mean by that crack? Sure I'm an Earthman."

All at once the anger, everything, seemed to go out of her. "I mean—I expected you to help me. But instead of that, you promised Koerber—" She couldn't go on.

"Now I get it. The note you slipped me. Look, sister, I haven't even had a chance to read it." Curt took it from his pocket and read it now. It was brief. *Please, you must help me! In the interests of justice, make no commitments to K. I shall contact you later and explain.*

"Darn. But look here, Dueela—what do you mean, 'in the interests of justice'? What have you to do with—with what Koerber's after?"

She did not answer at once. She had stepped to a dressing table, and now she came back with a jar of pale green unguent. Some of this she applied to Curt's neck, to a painful burn he was beginning to feel there.

"I'm sorry I had to use the parala-ray. But I was angry, furious with you."

"You did me a favor. At least I'm rid of Kraaz. You were listening outside Koerber's door?"

She nodded. Curt was aware of the perfumed nearness of her, the soft brush of her hair against his cheek. All at once his pulse seemed running away. He could not understand this. How could he feel…this…toward a murky skinned, sloe-eyed alien? He looked into her eyes then, looked deep, and saw the muddy brown flecked with gold. And he knew.

He gripped her arms fiercely, held her out from him. "You're not Ganymedian."

SHE twisted away, stood for a moment frightened. "I must trust you—I *must!*" Even her voice was different now. "You're not like Koerber, somehow I know you're not."

"Go on."

"I'm Terrestrial, too. I'm—Irene Landreth. Anton Landreth was my father. When he returned to Earth after that terrible mishap I tried my best to take care of him, to keep him with me. It—was pretty bad. Then he disappeared again, became the wanderer."

"Yes, I know," Curt said softly.

"Sometime later I learned that father was *here,* on Ganymede. I came here and learned other things. That horrible man Koerber had father, and was questioning him. Curt...I know that Koerber has a cerebra-scanner."

Curt's eyes went hard. Now the pattern was becoming clear. Koerber had said, "I spoke to Landreth shortly before he died." He hadn't mentioned *how* the man had died. The use of that terrible invention, the cerebra-scanner, was forbidden on all civilized planets. It extracted the cerebro-thalamic coordinates from a man's brain, arranged them into coherent pattern. And if used too far...

Curt stopped thinking of it, said: "Did your father ever mention—*The Silastah?*"

"Yes. But it doesn't mean anything to me, either. It meant something to him—something terrible, frightening."

"So the *Astrogar,*" Curt mused, "really belongs to you. And anything your father may have hidden on it. Is that right?"

The girl nodded. Curt came to his feet. "Irene, I'm going to follow this mystery to the end. Koerber thinks I'm working for him. Let him continue to think so. But I promise you—justice will be done."

"That's all I want. To clear father's name, to prove or disprove whatever he found out there. And one more thing." Her eyes went hard with knowing. "I've an idea how father died, here. Under the cerebro-scanner. But I haven't dared play my hand. Koerber may already suspect me."

"Yes, be careful. I think I can arrange for you to leave, inside of a day or two." Curt's eyes went about the room. "Are we still in the sub-city?"

"Yes, these are my quarters. Only a short distance from where Koerber is."

"Take me to the upper level, then. Where can I arrange to see you again?"

"The *Green Halo,* as before." With Irene leading the way, they came at last to more stairs leading up, then out into a cleverly concealed passage in the warehouse district. "I'll leave you here," she whispered. "Keep the parala-gun, you may need it."

BACK at his hotel, Curt felt a weariness upon him. The hour was late, but before retiring he examined the parala-ray gun, learned the secret of its operation.

Sleep would not come; his brain was too much in turmoil. In the morning he'd get his camera back. He'd cash that check of Koerber's, and there were other things to do. Already a plan was formulating...

He found himself thinking of Irene, marveling at the courage of this girl who would come here alone and get herself employed by such a dangerous man as Koerber. Her disguise was well nigh perfect, though.

A sharp knock at the door interrupted his thoughts. Curt was on his feet, flicked on the lights. He thrust the parala-gun beneath his mattress, then strode to the door, opened it cautiously.

Kraaz bulked there.

Curt sighed. "Okay, pal, come on. You sleep on the couch over there. I'll take the bed. Hope you don't snore." Kraaz complied, still grinning. He rubbed the back of his neck thoughtfully. Curt wondered how much Kraaz knew. He wished he could interpret that eternal Jovian grin.

CHAPTER FOUR

HE WAS no more enlightened the next day. For the most part Kraaz was silent and watchful, accompanying Curt everywhere on his trips about the city. But Curt had ceased to worry about Kraaz; he'd get rid of the big Jovian, all right, when the time came.

At the pretentious Interplanet Bank, the Ganymedian clerk didn't even raise an eyebrow as he paid out the small fortune in Credits which Koerber's check called for. Curt stuffed them into his wallet, grinned back at Kraaz.

"Now we can really operate, eh pal? Stick with me. I'll show you how it's done."

"Yez. Will be interezting."

Next, Curt redeemed his electro-camera from "The Shop of the Three Moons." From there they walked back to the main thoroughfare and stepped onto one of the Conveyers moving cross-town.

Curt debarked in front of a building with the scrolled insignia: *Tri-planet Space Shipping*. Kraaz followed him inside and listened indifferently as Curt demanded from a clerk:

"Let me see your Casualty Insurance Registers. Earth ships—about twelve years back." He made his voice crisply authoritative, at the same time flashing an enameled card that looked something like a Patrol identity card but wasn't.

The clerk wasn't fooled. He smiled thinly and shook his head. "Against regulations, sir. You know that. I can't—"

"Like the color of this better?" Curt slipped a twenty-credit note beneath the grill. The man palmed it, glanced quickly about. Then he jerked his head toward a swinging door.

"Down the hall, third room. I'll meet you there."

In the high-shelved room the clerk showed Curt the volumes he wanted. "Make it quick, will you, sir?" Curt nodded, went to work on the musty volumes, running a finger down the columns.

Absolute—Agfalon—Antares II—Astrogar. There it was. As easy as that. Curt read eagerly:

"*Astrogar: 200-ton, beryll.; 8-tube, 1000 max. displ.; mag-pl.; Perry-Linford, Chicago, Earth.*" Curt whistled softly.

"Perry-Linford. It was a darned good ship, then. Equipped with magni-plates too. It must have been one of the very first."

He read on. The *Astrogar* had cleared from Los Angeles, Earth, destination Turibek, Mars. Cleared from Turibek, Mars, destination X. And then—there it was. Found drifting two months later, 8000 miles below ecliptic, off Mars-Jupiter Space Lane 87. Damage to stern-jets, both magni-plates. Towed back to port of clearance, Earth. *Unclaimed in repair docks.* After nine months, as prescribed by law, sold at auction.

Sold to *Craigmyle,* Importers, Venus-Earth. Transformed into freighter. And there the information ended.

CURT'S lips curled down thoughtfully. Then he replaced the volume, pulled out a much later one. He turned to the supplement under *Venus.*

Luck was with him. Craigmyle, Inc. was listed and they had ten ships. One of them was the *Prince Taaran,* ex-*Stellar*—ex-*Astrogar.* Now it was 10-tube, same displacement, but with later-type magni-plates.

Curt followed the lead to still a later volume, and there the trail really came to an end. He bent closely over the page.

The *Prince Taaran*—which had once been *Astrogar*—had disappeared. It had been en route from Venus to Earth with a shipment of priceless Kra furs. Turning off course to avoid a space-vacuole, it had been halted by a barrage of vana-beams across the bow. Masked men had come aboard. They had set the crew adrift in lifeboats. The *Prince Taaran* had not been heard from since.

But what interested Curt was the date. This had happened scarcely four months ago.

Curt shut the volume softly, turned to see Kraaz watching him.

"What? You still here? Come on. I'm getting hungry."

He chose the Cafe *Karafel,* one of the city's ritziest. Kraaz was right beside him as they sat down at the table. The Jovian consumed his *ocelar*-steak dinner and looked as though he could enjoy another one, but Curt was too preoccupied now to be amazed. He settled the bill, and once more they boarded a Conveyer.

This time they headed downtown, toward the shopping center. Curt remained silent, thoughtful. The *Prince Taaran* and that hijacked shipment of Kra furs interested him. *Only four months ago.*

He entered one of the largest stores where he knew the personnel would be Terrestrial. The clerk who approached him was polished, suave. Curt selected a few small but expensive items and paid for them, making sure the man obtained a good glimpse of the large denomination Credits in his wallet. Then he added as an afterthought:

"Oh yes, I wanted something in furs. Something *nice,* you understand. You have something in Kra?"

The clerk was apologetic. "I'm very sorry, sir, they rarely reach us here on Ganymede. Perhaps something else? We've just received an importation of *Zaanth*-Martian, you know. They're exquisite, and coming into vogue."

Curt showed just the proper amount of annoyance. "Well...perhaps I'll look at them later. I'll be here for several weeks. If I could have your card?"

THE man was more than delighted. He handed Curt his engraved card. Kraaz was more than puzzled by all this, as they left the store. But Curt only smiled at him knowingly. He hadn't expected to find any Kra furs here; it was the card he really wanted. He would make good use of it.

Their next stop was the office of Interplanet Passenger Lines, where Curt learned a spacer was hoisting gravs for Earth in two days. This was luck. He quickly booked passage.

"For two," Kraaz reminded him, gripping his arm fiercely.

"What?" Curt looked at the big Jovian. "Oh, yes. I mustn't forget *you*, Kraaz." He paid out more money for another ticket, thinking what a waste it was. The ticket he had bought was for Irene Landreth, not himself. Curt had no intention of returning to Earth for quite a while.

Evening was coming on, as they leisurely strolled the boulevard. Jupiter thrust its bulk along the horizon, long reddish shadows falling before it. Curt glanced sidelong at Kraaz. It was time to get rid of him now.

By this time the big Jovian was thoroughly baffled. He could contain himself no longer. Frowning, he turned to Curt.

"The trail of the *Astrogar*—it leadz back to Earth?"

"Figure it out for yourself, Sherlock. I'm not giving away my trade secrets."

"Zherlock? What iz—"

"Skip it, you wouldn't understand." They paused at one of the mono-car stations, where the crowds were waiting for transportation cross-town. At two-minute intervals the cars came, gyros humming softly. The large *duraplon* gate slid back. The crowd surged forward. Red lights flashed, and the gate closed again. Curt was fascinated. He stood aside and watched. Silently he counted off the seconds. The operation was precise as clockwork.

Kraaz fidgeted. At last he grasped Curt's arm. "We go back to hotel now—not?"

"Not," Curt said. "I've one more trip to make. Have to take a car. Come on."

They moved forward with the crowd. Curt stayed close to the wall, managed to maneuver Kraaz on the other side of him. They neared the gate as the first red light flashed. At that precise instant Curt fell back, hugged the wall.

He'd timed it just right. Kraaz was carried forward with the last second surge. His bulk was nothing to that mob. Kraaz found himself shoved through the gate, tried to whirl back but too late. It slid shut against him; the time lock clicked into place.

Curt stood on the outside, grinning at the big Jovian whose brows had arched up into astonished punctuation marks. Then a mask of fury darkened Kraaz' features. He rattled out a string of oaths, exhausted what he knew in English, then continued in his own language.

"Too bad, pal," Curt waved cheerily. "But this is goodbye. In any language."

CURT wasted no time. He hurried back toward those streets bordering the spaceport, and at last found the sub-level saloon, the *Green Halo*.

It was still early. He found a table in a far corner, but commanding a view of both doors. Kraaz wasn't so slow between the ears that he might not think of this place again. But Curt's concern now was for Irene Landreth. She had seemed worried last night—more so than she wanted Curt to realize.

He ordered Martian *laajra* and sipped at it slowly, as he watched the evening patrons enter the place: Martians from the mines, Earthmen from the freighters, and a few eager-eyed tourists who entered and ordered a drink and then left the place hurriedly. For there was a brooding atmosphere here of things violent and unknown, which settled over the place like a patina.

If only the girl would hurry. More than an hour had passed, and Curt was sipping at his third drink, when he suddenly saw her. She merely appeared in the doorway at the rear, and glanced about the smoke-filled room. Her glance crossed his but didn't linger. Then she was gone.

Curt gave her five minutes, then rose and moved through the rear door. No one challenged him. Irene was waiting for him, where the secret stone stairway led down. And not until they were once more in the subterranean city, did she speak.

"Koerber's found out, about me—I'm sure of it. He sent one of his men to make inquiries at the Employment Bureau. In a few days he'll know my credentials were forged."

"By that time," Curt reassured her, "you won't be here."

"You've—made progress?"

"Of a sort. The trail of the *Astrogar* vanishes, but I'm playing a hunch. I think I'll pick up the trail again on Ceres. But I want you to go back to Earth and await word from me. Give me one month, and I guarantee you'll have the *Astrogar.*"

"No. You don't understand. I'm following the trail too, wherever it leads. I don't know why you say *Ceres,* but that's good enough for me."

Something about her voice, and the firm line of her chin there in the semidarkness, stopped Curt's protests. "All right," he shrugged. "Ceres will be dangerous, but—at least you're better company than Kraaz." He stopped abruptly. "Where are we going now?"

"I haven't been idle either," she said. "I know where Koerber keeps his private cruiser. It's a fine ship, and kept ready at all times for emergency trips."

"Marvelous! After all, Koerber told me to spare no expenses, didn't he?" Curt smiled at her, and felt his admiration for this girl grow apace within him.

THEY came at last to an extensive area, where they saw a few sprawling, well-lighted buildings. The clang of metal on metal reached their ears, and the faint hiss of atomic furnaces.

"Things go on here that the Patrol would like to know about." Irene said. "Koerber has a well-organized crew, both here and in the space-lanes."

They kept to the shadows, and skirted these buildings. Curt eased the parala-gun from his belt and held it ready.

"Know how to use that?" Irene whispered.

"Maybe not as well as you," Curt grinned, "but I'll keep it anyway. Guards around Koerber's ship?"

"I'm not sure. Be ready, anyway. We're almost there." She pointed to a lone, low-structured building ahead. It was dark. But they waited, listening, peering through the gloom. No sound reached them. They crept forward. They reached a corner of the building unchallenged and Curt found a door, fumbled along the edge of it. He pressed a stud and the door went up with a groan that sent harrowing echoes into the night.

They waited, breathless. But the damage had been done. Already a figure was leaping around the building's corner toward them. Curt whirled to meet the Jovian guard's rush. He brought up his hand just in time, and released the parala-ray. The guard crumpled, but not before his hand flew to his mouth and a shrill note echoed away.

Now other men, Earthmen and Jovians, were racing from the nearby shops. Curt knew he couldn't stop all of them, even with a parala-ray. He whirled to find Irene, but she was gone. Then he heard her voice from inside the door.

"Curt, hurry! Here's the ship!"

They gained the trim, black cruiser and stumbled into the lock just as Koerber's men gained the outer door. Curt threw his weight against a lever. The ship's lock clicked into place behind him.

"They have ato-beams," Irene gasped. "If they blast in here—"

But already Curt was racing forward, toward the control console. His eyes flicked over the controls. Some he knew, but others were strange to him. No time to waste now. He went to work, lights flicked on and the rocket feeds hummed. Already they could hear the sing of ato-beams at work on the ship's *duralloy* doors.

"No time to look for the exit now." Curt muttered. "Hold on."

Rocket-flame surged. The spacer leaped forward like a monster unleashed, taking the entire side of the building with it in a splintering sound. Curt peered into the forward V-Panel, and sighed with relief. They had entered a vast underground tunnel, illumined by the spacer's beam. Their speed was constant now, and remained so despite Curt's efforts at the controls.

AGAIN he peered forward. Huge spiraling coils were banked at intervals on either side of the tunnel.

"Synchronized magnetic fields to minimize acceleration. But I wonder where this tunnel leads? Must come out on the surface of Ganymede somewhere."

Ten minutes later the tunnel veered sharply upward. Suddenly the magnetic fields were gone and they burst into the night sky, from high in the Naaric Range that straddled half of Ganymede. Far below and to the south sprawled the winking lights of Ganymede City.

"Only Koerber could have thought this one up." Curt exclaimed. Then he was at the navigator's table, making calculations for the erratic orbit of Ceres. He checked the figures twice, finally locked the anti-grav sheaths into place.

"Ceres," Irene breathed, watching over his shoulder. "Oh, I hope you're right. If we find the *Astrogar* there it will…"

Curt glanced up. For a long moment their eyes met in delighted silence. Then the spell was broken, as a harsh voice cut in:

"We are in free zpaze at lazt? Good!"

Curt whirled, gained his feet as Kraaz towered in the control-room door. Kraaz wasn't grinning now. Nor was he buying any more of that parala-ray. Curt had the gun only half out of his belt when the Jovian was upon him. The gun clattered to the floor and Curt hit the opposite wall with stunning force, as Kraaz thrust out a huge hand.

Kraaz picked up the gun then bulked in the center of the room, ignoring the Earth girl in the guise of a Ganymedian. He moved over to the slowly tracing chart— stood studying it.

Curt came up from the floor. He sagged against the wall, shook his head like a punch-drunk fighter. Through ringing ears he heard Kraaz' voice.

"Zo. It iz Zerez, our deztination. Good. That iz very good."

CHAPTER FIVE

CERES came up in the panel like a dark whirling juggernaut. Thirty hours had passed and Curt was once more at the controls. But Kraaz stood by, ever watchful, and now he had the parala-gun.

The ruse had been simple, Kraaz explained. Koerber was aware of Irene Landreth's identity, also knew that she had contacted Curt and might make a try for his private cruiser. So Kraaz had stationed himself in the cruiser to await their coming. It had all worked out beautifully.

Curt grimaced now as he thought of it, and other things. What was the secret of the *Astrogar?* Had Koerber extracted that secret from Landreth's mind? Curt was sure of one thing now: Koerber would stop at nothing to get that ship, and Kraaz would not be shaken again.

He leaned forward to watch the hundred-mile diameter of Ceres rushing up to meet them. Irene stood tense with excitement, and now she voiced the question she had been wanting to ask:

"Curt…why Ceres? Everyone knows it's nothing but an airless world of rock…"

Curt shook his head, grasped the magni-viewfinder and swung it in wide parabolas. A dark ragged terrain was spreading out below them. Then, Curt saw the place at last. A deep gorge, with cliffs towering up on either side. He'd only been here twice before in his life but he knew the place well.

He maneuvered into place, and the cruiser descended slowly on the under-hull repulse beam. Even Kraaz was puzzled now, as they went deep into this tiny world. Suddenly the scene widened. The terrain spread out again and lights leaped into view. They were in a vast hollow where a complete town nestled, concealed by the sheering black cliffs. They settled dawn onto a spaceport where a hundred ships rested.

"Welcome to Ceres," Curt spoke dryly. "But I hope we won't be staying long." He glanced at Irene. "It'll be safer if you stay here with the ship, while Kraaz and I take a look around."

The big Jovian nodded. They stepped down into the thin atmosphere of Ceres' depths. Ships of all sizes and designs rested there in the vast hollow; for this was an outlaw base for pirates of all planets. They came as they pleased, setting down for a few weeks or months, then leaving for places unknown and unasked. Not one man in a million knew of this place. Certainly the Tri-Planet Patrol didn't.

"How you know of thiz plaze?" Kraaz asked curiously.

Curt shrugged and was silent. Men didn't ask questions here, nor answer them. This much he knew: their lives were forfeit if their mission became known. Carefully they wended their way in darkness, among the scores of ships.

"I'll tell you this, Kraaz. The *Astrogar* will now be the *Prince Taaran*—ten-tube, with latest type magni-plates fore and aft. Keep your eyes peeled for such a ship."

They saw spacers of every description, from the tiny solar-powered Mercurian cruisers, to the plodding Callistan freighters. There were Earth ships aplenty, but they failed to meet the description Curt was after. But suddenly, as they neared the edge of the hollow—he saw one. He grasped Kraaz' arm and headed that way. The presence of the big Jovian was comforting now. If they were challenged...

Curt's hopes rose, as they neared the spacer and made out the design. It was Earthian all right, sleek and slim with a suggestion of speed. Painted solid black. There were the ten rear tubes, arranged circularly. There were the magni-plates fore and aft, seeming powerful enough to shunt good-sized meteors away. This might be the *Astrogar!*

CURT walked forward, looking up at the circular ports. All were dark. He reached the prow, looked up for the name and saw it emblazoned: LUCIFER.

His hopes were dashed. But something drew Curt back, held him there. And suddenly he knew. He unhooked the electro-camera from his belt, set the dial for the penetro-beam. This would be dangerous, flashing a light around a strange ship—but he had to chance it. He turned the powerful beam upward, played it across the name LUCIFER.

His heart leaped. A great square patch had been newly painted there, and beneath that patch his beam picked out the old letters: PRINCE TAARAN.

They'd found it at last. If this ship had once been the *Prince Taaran*—it was also the *Astrogar!*

Kraaz had seen. Now he strode purposefully toward the side locks. It took all of Curt's strength on his arm to stop him.

"Careful, man. Remember you're on Ceres Base now." Curt jerked his head toward the lights of the town. "The owner must be around somewhere—let's go find him."

Kraaz nodded. They walked toward the single sprawling street of Ceres Base. Sounds of revelry reached them, guttural laughter and curses and the click of gambling wheels. Once they saw a thin, blue flash of an electro-pistol. That was the only law here, and life was cheap among these cutthroat pirates.

They entered a place that seemed the largest and noisiest in the town. Through a blue fog of smoke Curt saw that Sonneson was still behind the bar, and that was a break. Sonneson remembered him—but not as Curt Vaughn.

"Hello, Doc. What'll it be this time?" It was as though he'd seen Curt only yesterday, instead of a year ago.

"The same. Nothing for my friend, here."

"The zame, too," Kraaz spoke—and Curt looked at him in amazement.

"Don't tell me you're going to take a drink for once in your misbegotten life!"

"Maybe will need, tonight." Kraaz was ill at ease here. Sonneson returned just then with the bourbon. Curt nodded approvingly and said to Kraaz:

"See what a memory he has? A year since I was here, but he remembers I called for good Earth bourbon."

Sonneson's lips pulled back in a greasy smile. "That's because it beats all these other heathen drinks. But I do have a good memory."

"Do you now?" Curt said softly as he poured from the bottle. "Then I wonder if you remember who brought in the LUCIFER."

SONNESON'S fat face went blank and he started to move away, quick. Curt reached across the bar and gripped him.

"Strictly business. There'll be no trouble for *you*." At the same time, Curt shoved a ten-credit note forward.

Sonneson took the note, wet his lips nervously. "Tarnuff brought in the LUCIFER. He's been here quite a while now. I think he has a shipment of furs."

"We both think so. Tarnuff, eh? He's Martian?"

"Yeah. Be careful, Doc, he's a mean one."

"Show me a Martian who isn't."

"I'll show you Tarnuff. That's him over there." The bartender nodded toward a far table where a group of Martians were sitting. There was no mistaking Tarnuff; he was the biggest and ugliest of the group, and he did the talking while the others listened.

"Thanks, Sonneson. See you again a year from now."

The bartender said meaningfully, "I hope so," but already Curt and Kraaz were crossing to the Martians' table.

Curt changed his style now. He stood there hesitant, and made his voice meek:

"Pardon me, gentlemen. I—uh—understand one of you is named Tarnuff?"

Tarnuff leaned back, hooked his thumbs in his belt. "Who wants to know?"

"Well…I—" Curt was fumbling at his pocket. Instantly three electro-pistols showed across the top of the table. Curt gulped.

"I only wanted to show you my card!" He drew out the engraved card he'd obtained from the clerk on Ganymede City. He extended it to Tarnuff.

Tarnuff flicked it to the floor, and his face grew ugly. "Who sent you here? Koerber? We don't like the way he's been sticking his nose in here, trying to organize the independents."

"Koerber?" Curt made his voice puzzled. "I never heard of *him*. I'm a buyer for the Nardon Bros., Furriers. I understood I would find a shipment of Kra…" He looked regretfully down at the card.

Tarnuff picked up the card and looked at it. His frown smoothed out. "Hmm. Nardon Bros." His eyes flicked to Kraaz. "And who is this?"

"My superiors assigned him to me as a guide here. I have been authorized, sir, to buy your entire shipment. If we can come to terms?" Curt was fumbling with his wallet, now, revealing its content. Then he glanced nervously about the room. "If we could repair to the privacy of your ship? I—I shouldn't want to talk business here, anything might happen…"

"You're right, this is a dangerous place. By all means let us go to my ship." A look of cunning had crept into Tarnuff's eyes. He stood up, and Curt didn't miss the furtive little signal he gave the other three Martians.

TARNUFF led the way, back to the spaceport and through the maze of ships to the LUCIFER. He didn't seem bothered by Kraaz' presence, and Curt saw why; an electro bulged beneath the Martian's space-tunic. Curt knew that once this man got them aboard, he'd blast them both down in cold blood.

They paused at the side lock. Tarnuff turned a key in the complicated mechanism. A door swung down, formed a little flight of stairs. Tarnuff motioned Curt to enter. Curt started up the steps, smiling; for he'd caught an imperceptible nod from Kraaz.

He glimpsed Kraaz starting to follow. Then the big Jovian took a sidling step, and a powerful arm was around Tarnuff's throat. Curt whirled and leaped downward, but already Kraaz had borne the Martian to the ground. It was over quickly, silently. Tarnuff lay quite still and it was obvious his neck was broken.

Kraaz held up a hand. "Lizzen!"

Footsteps were approaching. Quickly they grasped Tarnuff, dragged him beneath the hull, out of the light spilling down. They crouched there in darkness and watched the other three Martians approach. Kraaz whispered, "Now!"

The element of surprise was theirs. Curt bore one of them down, took a knee to the midriff as the man fought back. But Curt drove blindly, felt his fists connect. At last the Martian went limp beneath him. He winced as he heard a sound nearby that could have been skulls cracking together; then he saw Kraaz straightening up.

"We make a good team, Kraaz."

"Yez. We have the *Aztrogar* now. Go back to other zhip, get Mizz Landreth."

For an instant Curt hesitated, then decided Kraaz wouldn't pull a double-cross at this late date. Soon he was back with Irene, and a few minutes later they were lifting far from Ceres, where they fell into a free orbit. Kraaz had all the weapons now, including the electro he'd lifted from Tarnuff. Surprisingly enough, he now handed the latter weapon to Curt.

Curt watched this Jovian. There was something strange about the man—strange and unpredictable. Kraaz spoke at last, facing them:

"Zo. We have the *Aztrogar.* But I think not we take it to Koerber yet—eh? What iz zecret of the *Aztrogar?*"

Curt shrugged, watching the man's expressionless features. Kraaz turned to the girl.

"You know zecret, Mizz Landreth?"

"No. I used to know this ship well, but I've never been aboard since—since father brought it back from that awful trip to the asteroids." She shuddered, glanced around. "It—it seems different now, somehow."

"IT'S passed through several hands," Curt reminded. "Naturally there'd be changes of cabins, remodeling, new equipment...Kraaz, tell me something. Ever hear the word *Silastah?*"

He'd expected to take the Jovian unawares. But the latter's eyes were puzzled.

"Zilaztah," he pronounced it. "No, that word meanz nothing to me. But the zecret of *Aztrogar* iz here—aboard. I am zure of it, and we zhall find it."

It wasn't that easy. Curt set the automatic controls, and there followed the weariest two hours any of them had experienced. They went through the ship from stem to stern. They examined everything—controls, cabins, tool lockers, the air units, anti-gravs, inner and outer locks. They even dismantled the tube-feeds and rocket heads. They sounded the walls for hidden compartments. They took precise measurements. And they sank down at last, in utter weariness.

"The outzide?" Kraaz suggested.

Curt shook his head. "No. It's here. We've overlooked something. Hell, we don't even know what we're looking *for!* Whatever it is, it's been hidden here, for ten years."

"This just can't be the *Astrogar,*" Irene spoke. "It's— too different."

"I know spaceships, and spacer construction. There's no mistaking a Perry-Linford ship—" Curt suddenly brightened. "I forgot one thing. At least I can prove this is the right ship. Should have thought of it before."

He led the way to the engine room. He bent beneath the singing coils, looked long and hard at the *duralloy* block that encased the inter-ship gravity rotors. They'd looked there before. But now Curt rubbed away the dirt and grime, the accumulation of a decade. Letters appeared, stamped into the metal itself. PERRY-LINFORD, CHICAGO. And beneath it: *Astrogar.*

But there was something else. There was a thin seam of metal, newer and different metal. Curt drew in his breath sharply. "An atomic weld. Holy roaring comets, this is it! Sure, there'd be a hiding place inside this block, beneath the rotors. Kraaz...go back to the tool lockers, bring me a thin-gauge cutting beam."

Soon the beam was searing through the block, following the line of the old weld. A ten-inch section fell away. Curt reached far beneath the spherical rotors, fumbling. At last his fingers encountered something. Gradually he eased it forward, drew it out.

He held a flat, ten-inch disc of *duraplon*—a container of some sort.

ONCE more in the control room, they examined the find curiously. There was no inscription of any kind on the container. Curt managed to get the lid off. There was a reel of thin, very thin metal. And scratched into the metallic strip was a series of unbroken but eccentric lines.

"This is an early type directional finder. The one thing that will give us the exact location of Landreth's asteroid. Sure—I get it now. Koerber knew this was hidden here, he must have learned that when he had Landreth under the cerebro-scanner..." Curt stopped short, looked at Irene whose face had gone white beneath the Ganymedian tan.

"I'm sorry, Irene, but we've got to review this in perspective. Look—get this picture. Your father was drifting for weeks before the Patroller found him. He was slowly going crazy. But he retained enough of sanity to hide this 'finder' away. Why did he do that?"

Kraaz answered. "Becauze he found treazure there, vazt treazure—and he wanted zome day to go back."

"I don't believe that, Kraaz, and I don't think you believe it. Maybe Koerber does. No...there are wild stories Landreth told, about a menace that could some day threaten the structure of the entire System..."

Kraaz' lips pulled back in a grin. "Zo Landreth hid hiz 'finder,' to prevent other men from retracing hiz route and dizcovering what he dizcovered. But you, Curt Vaughn—you believe theze ztoriez?"

"Hell, man—who knows what to believe?" He looked suspiciously at Kraaz. "What about you?"

"I only know thiz. We do not go back to Koerber. We make uze of thiz directional-finder and go to Landreth'z azteroid—eh?"

"No. That's out." It's what Curt wanted to do too, but he was thinking of Irene now.

"Curt, Kraaz is right! If father did find something there, we can take back proof. I thought you were a Newsman, and this is News! Besides, the *Astrogar* is legally mine, and that makes me commander, and—"

"And you're a little fool," Curt grated. "All right. I'm out-commanded and out-voted."

He went to work with the directional-finder, setting up a circuit through which the metal tape fed, this in turn giving proper electrical impulse to the rocket-feeds.

"Ceres is constant," he explained, "and Landreth crossed its orbit. We'll have to pick up the trail from that. It's going to be ticklish."

FOR hours he worked over the "finder," making adjustments of speed and direction, correlating it to the ink-lined chart being traced on the navigator's table. The movement of the tape through the electrical feed was hardly perceptible now, but every inch of it meant a rocket-thrust of hundreds of miles.

"That's it." Curt straightened up at last. "We're on the trail Landreth followed, and I'd say it should bring us into the belt about forty hours from now. You know we're already off any of the established space-lanes, don't you?"

They knew it too well. And it was borne ever more upon them as the hours passed, and they sped into darkness. True, men had gone into the asteroids and emerged. There were charted swarms, with established routes to reach them. But the belt covered vast reaches, and they were going into the uncharted.

They took their turns at sleep, and at the controls. Irene proved adept. Already Curt was beginning to regret this move, as Irene came to sit in the control seat beside him. He'd done crazy things like this before, of course, but that had been different. He'd done them alone. This girl...

He turned to look at her; his eyes widened. "I've been wondering when you were going to do that."

"Do what?"

"Fix your hair back to Earth style, and your eyes. Quite an improvement."

"Yes, I suppose it is." Her mind was elsewhere—she was worried. "That Kraaz is a strange man..."

"Strange?" Curt laughed harshly. "He's more than strange, he's an enigma. First he's working for Koerber, then he isn't. Or is he? Darned if I know any more. I think he knows more about this deal than he pretends."

"He frightens me sometimes."

"He'd frighten anyone. Keep your eye on him; I don't trust him yet. At least," Curt tapped the electro at his belt, "I feel better having this."

They peered at the vast emptiness reflected in the V-Panel. Soon that space wouldn't be empty; it would be too crowded for comfort. Curt turned the magni-lens dial. Tiny flecks of light appeared far ahead. He consulted the chart.

"That'll be the Lanisar Group, I guess. We're getting into the Belt."

It came upon them fast. There was no need to skirt it. Dark masses loomed about them, some of the larger pieces forming miniature solar systems in themselves. Others veered in eccentric orbits, hurtling across their bow, seeming much closer than they actually were. The *Astrogar's* repulsion plates kept them away.

Curt nodded in satisfaction. Men had died out here, charting and exploring these swarms, before there had been such things as repulsion plates.

OTHER swarms followed the Lanisar Group. Endless masses, spinning and pockmarked, reflecting the leprous sunlight. It was harrowing, but Curt was used to this. The worst would come. It was coming already, as the directional tape caused the rockets to swing their trajectory ever inward, toward uncharted regions.

Kraaz relieved him, and Irene prepared food and coffee, which they'd found in the well-stocked larder. Curt tried to catch a few hours sleep, but now a restlessness was upon him. Already they'd passed close to several rocks of twenty-mile diameter; the repulsion plates were doing well to hold.

And now the directional-finder was nearing the end. Curt was sure his adjustments of it had been correct, and they'd soon be there. Be where? X. Asteroid-X, the unknown. What had Anton Landreth found there? Sure, the man had come out half-crazed, and Curt was convinced it wasn't entirely space-madness. Another thing—why had Landreth wanted to return?

"*Silastah.*" Curt found himself thinking of that word again, and he pronounced it aloud. It had a curious, lingering sibilance. Surely Landreth must have heard that word *here*. Did that mean there were creatures here, living things? But that was impossible. Life on the asteroids—

His thoughts stopped abruptly. There came a rending crash, followed by a lurch that threatened to tear the ship asunder. Curt was flung from the bunk, lay momentarily dazed against the opposite wall. He groped for the door...managed to stagger into the outer corridor. The *Astrogar* was still spinning wildly.

"We're there!" Kraaz was shouting from the control seat. "It'z a big one—gravity tore ztern platez looze." He was tugging mightily at the controls. Curt managed to reach him, but their combined strength was not enough to hold off that gravity.

"The starboard repulsors!" Curt yelled. "Blast! Blast to starboard!"

Already Kraaz was doing that. Slowly the ship heeled around so the repulsors could take effect. It helped, but it wasn't enough. A great dark mass was surging below them now, coming up fast, with jagged pinnacles reaching out and deep black gullies agape.

They neared the surface on a long tangent. Kraaz made a last mighty effort to bring the prow up. The *Astrogar* touched rock, veered wildly, ploughed forward with a rending of metal that could only mean the under-hull was being sheared away. They had arrived on X.

CHAPTER SIX

IRENE emerged from a stateroom, dazed but unhurt. Kraaz was lifting himself from the tangle of the control-board, dabbing at his cheek where blood was coming down. Curt crossed over to the directional-finder. The device had been unerring, the tape had run its course. This was undoubtedly Landreth's asteroid. And then—Curt saw something else.

He bent quickly, fingered two thin wires attached to the electrical feed. He hadn't put those wires there. They didn't belong there.

Quick he followed their course, along the floor paneling, cleverly concealed, up to the little alcove housing the ship's Tele-sender. Curt had examined this Sender before, and thought it was out of order. But now it clicked away softly, sending out its code. Angrily he ripped the wires away, turned to face Kraaz.

"You rat, you did this! Where's that message going?"

Kraaz shrugged. "Too late. Iz already gone—ever zince we crozzed orbit of Lanizar."

"I said where!"

"Code penetratez ether, even to Ganymede. Koerber pickz it up on zuper-zenzitive rezeiver, our route iz telezcribed onto another 'directional' tape. Koerber then comez here, in very powerful zhip...knowz route iz zafe..."

Curt listened to this, his face going white with anger. "I get it. So this was Koerber's plan all the time. Now he has the location of this asteroid by proxy. I was beginning to think you were okay, Kraaz, but it seems I was wrong—you're still playing in with Koerber!" Curt choked, trying to find more words.

"Doez not matter now. Iz done. Koerber payz me well, I do the job." Kraaz was serene, dabbing at his cut face. "Maybe iz well if Koerber doez come—eh? We are wrecked, and if we ever expect to leave here—"

"Yeah. I might have known Koerber would play it safe. We do the dirty work, to make sure the route's safe for him."

"At leazt, there iz zufficient air here," Kraaz indicated the register. "Alzo gravity is heavy. We may az well examine the damage."

The towering, serrated cliffs were far from reassuring, and the soil of the narrow valley had a poisonous, deadly look. It seemed slightly iridescent. The atmosphere was tenuous.

"Pretty much of a mess." Curt said acidly as they examined the length of the ship's hull that was sheared open. "Maybe we can patch it up, though."

"At leazt we will try. Give uz zomething to do until Koerber comez."

They dragged a few beryloid strips from the storage lockers. Curt went to work setting up the portable atomic furnace, and Kraaz used his tremendous strength to advantage, trying to twist the torn repulsion plate back into shape. Then, while Curt worked with the nozzle, Irene operated the atomic flow according to his directions.

IT was slow and disheartening work, but it kept their minds off the vague shadowy vistas stretching around them. Out there lay madness. Already they had caught a feeling of it—a feeling of something. There were scarcely heard *whisperings* that seemed to press in, no more than the shadow of thoughts. Yet no wind was here, and nothing moved.

More than once Curt stopped to stare around, cocked his head in an attitude of listening. And the whisperings stopped, to resume again a moment later. He tried to shrug off the feeling that something was nearby, watching—curious.

"Irene, bring me a smaller-gauge nozzle—this one won't do much longer." Sweat was streaming from him despite the night chill. He saw the girl turn, head for the ship's lock. Then he heard her scream.

She was standing quite still. Curt hurried beside her, stared to where she pointed. Close to the ground, around the end of the ship, came something. It was merely a shape, blacker than the black night of this asteroid. It surged toward them with an almost-protoplasmic motion, constantly changing shape. Then, with a distinct shock, Curt saw that no part of it touched the ground at all.

Curt reached down, adjusted the charge on the atomic nozzle. More of the shapes were coming now. They were half the size of a man and they drifted—mere blobs of blackness, seeming quite substanceless. But now there was something else. Within those shapes flashed a fine network of lines—blue, erratic, dancing—seemingly, an electrical charge.

Curt waited for no more. He leveled the atomic nozzle, released the charge. It caught the nearest shape, sent it buffeting back as though on a gust of wind. The shape spun merrily for a moment, then came on, faster, pressed by the others. Curt heard Kraaz shouting from the other end of the ship. Apparently he'd encountered them too.

"Irene—quickly. Get to the lock! I'll try to hold them off."

But it was too late for that. The blobs of blackness came sliding down the ship's hull, cutting off their retreat. Curt swung the nozzle around. One of the shapes sped forward, touched his arm. There was a tingling shock, not unpleasant, then the nozzle dropped from his nerveless fingers. He swung wildly with his free hand, saw that Irene was lashing out against them too.

"Curt…they're *nothing*. My hand passes clear through them!"

It was true. Curt had the feeling that he was battling black substanceless ghosts. Black ghosts. The thought struck him as ludicrous and he laughed a bit wildly…then one of them touched him on the neck and he couldn't move a muscle. Irene, too, seemed unable to move now.

"Don't fight theze things." came Kraaz' booming voice. "No uze. We zhall zee what they want." A moment later he came into view, surrounded by a score of the shapes.

THE paralysis soon passed. Then they started walking, prodded forward by those electrical charges, which could be painful. Curt looked back regretfully at the spaceship. But the shapes herded them ever onward, toward the end of this long valley, toward the jutting cobalt cliffs. Curt thought grimly that this must be the way Anton Landreth had gone.

The way was hard. The floor of the valley fell downward into a rocky chasm, with cliffs rearing on all sides. The three were silent, giving all their attention to the dangerous footing. But at last the way leveled out, and Curt muttered:

"These things have a modicum of intelligence. They seem to be a manifestation of pure energy, pure force." He reached out, tried to touch the black shapes pressing close to him. Beyond a slight tingling, his hand felt nothing. He stood quite still, demanded aloud: "Where are you taking us?"

There came no answer except an intensification of the energy-flow, which galvanized Curt to motion.

"Had better take it eazy," Kraaz warned. "Theze thingz may have a terrific potenzial."

The way led further into the rock. The walls began to widen out. And now the fluctuating blue lines, within the energy-shapes, began to dance wildly. Curt could sense an excitement here. There came a sort of mass sighing, as if the shapes were in tenuous communication. The sighing became more pronounced, evolved into a sibilant chant that rose and died and rose again. Curt cocked his head, listening.

"Silastah," the chant seemed to say.

"Si-las-tah…" Only that, over and over again. And there was awe in it—awe and a sort of reverence.

Curt felt a chill come over him.

Now they were moving at a more cautious pace. Irene moved close to Curt, and he felt her trembling. The chant continued to go up from their captors. Suddenly, light appeared ahead, a sparkling leaping light that seemed to emanate from a vast grotto opening before them. At the very brink of this grotto the black energy-shapes came to a halt, massing tightly about the three.

"Si-las-tah…" The chant surged up once more, a bit frantically. Then, as though at a given signal, the shapes broke apart. They went wildly spinning, careening, back along the way they had come.

Speechless, the three stared after them until they disappeared into darkness. Kraaz spoke at last, his voice not quite steady. "I—I don't like thiz. Why they leave uz?"

"Why?" Curt's voice echoed wildly about the walls. "I have a feeling we've been—*delivered.* You know, like three pieces of baggage."

THE grotto yawned before them. It stretched for unimaginable distances, a place of shimmering, iridescent beauty. The walls in every direction sent forth clashing colors of light, until the place seemed filled with a rainbow mist. Heaps of faceted crystal lay scattered about. Stalactites in every size reared up from the floor, reached out from the walls. Nothing was here but color and crystalline confusion.

"Come on," Curt said. He stepped down a rough-hewn stairway.

From the lower vantage they could see tunnels leading away into similar caverns. But they seemed more like streets than tunnels—well kept and symmetrically designed. And now, as they stood staring around, a *presence* seemed to beat upon them. It was just that, an all-pervading presence. There came a growing conviction that they were under surveillance. A thousand unseen eyes seemed watching them. A thousand ghostly fingers seemed probing away softly, delicately at their minds.

"It's this damned light," Curt tried to make his voice reassuring. "Radioactive maybe." But he knew it wasn't that. Something else was here—very close.

Irene gasped, clutched at Curt's arm. She was staring at the floor ahead of her, pointing with a trembling finger.

"It moved. Curt, I saw it move!"

Then they all saw it. It was like a nightmare come to life. One of the glittering crystal heaps had indeed moved. Now it was shifting, rearranging itself, rearing itself up. They stood rooted there, staring as though sanity had left them. They saw the tiny crystals cling together with a peculiar cohesion, saw the entire mass arise, glittering, shifting, taking on the rough semblance of a man.

"STEADY now, steady." Curt gripped the girl's arm, heard her dry sobs and knew she was on the edge of hysteria. He turned and saw other crystalline masses behind them, taking on the roughly human semblance. Scores of them were coming into being, moving up from the floor, sliding down from the walls.

The forms moved in, with lumbering steps. Crystal facet moved against facet, setting up an eternal tinkling sound. Curt's electro-blast was in his hand now. He sprayed the beam around but it was useless, sputtering harmlessly against those nightmare shapes. Kraaz was trying too, with the parala-ray—but that was futile.

The entities were aglow with a deep inner light. They raised heavy appendages. Tiny crystals slid forward to become tentacles, grasping the three visitors by the arms. Those tentacles were heavy and strong and cold, cold as outer space. Kraaz struggled, lashing out with his Jovian strength. But mere protoplasmic strength was nothing. His great muscles bulged, veins stood out—then he collapsed.

THEY were dragged roughly forward, through street after street in which other crystalline forms moved. But not all were in human semblance. They seemed able to take on any shape at will. A tingling din was set up, as these crystal-shapes moved in their peculiar cohesive locomotion.

An entire city seemed to exist here far beneath the asteroid rock. They came at last into another grotto, vaster than any they'd seen. Their captors led them to a great blank wall of rock, extending far above their heads. But it wasn't entirely blank, hundreds of crystal forms clustered there, scattered in profusion across the perpendicular expanse.

As they stood there uncertainly, these crystal-forms began to move. Slowly, a vast pattern began to form across the wall. It seemed purposeful and deliberate. A pattern of super-imposed circles, triangles, and other perfect geometric shapes, forming at last a single entity of surpassing beauty. And this Entity was intelligent. Curt knew it at once, even before an inner light came forth, shattering through the millions of facets.

A bit of the light focused, reached out-enveloped them. Curt steeled himself against it. It was cold but not at all unpleasant. The light probed for a moment, seemed to intensify. Then came a clear mental impression:

"Yes. I find that your life-base is...protoplasmic. Long ago, another such one came here."

Irene went tense. "It means—father," she whispered.

The probing went on. "I find you are startled at discovering our life-form here. Why should that be? Your life-base is... carbon. Ours is silicic. The sustaining principle behind both is similar and universal: electrical force-energy. We are mobile, we absorb nourishment, we propagate our kind, we have a system of science and mathematics. Ours was once a great civilization—and will be again." There came a surge of pride. "I believe us to be a manifestation of the *pure* life-form, the precise and the flawless—the ultimate."

The great crystal-entity shifted, taking on new colors and patterns, as the three absorbed what it had said. Curt started to speak, but was interrupted:

"Do not—*speak,* protoplasmic one. Project thought-patterns. I will intuit."

Curt concentrated, managed to envision the thought: *you say you absorb nourishment. What, and how?*

"You are very perceiving. But I shall answer you. Our means of subsistence stems from the energy-source that you call electronic, or to be more precise, the free energy resulting from the disintegration of *metal*. Yes, metal becomes scarce here; we have had to burrow deep in search of it. Soon we must leave this world...expand..."

Curt suddenly knew what this silicic creature meant. He remembered Landreth's incoherent stories, about a menace out here that could become a threat to the entire System.

BUT again the thoughts were coming, taking such relentless hold of his mind that he reeled under them.

"Tell me, protoplasmic one...I know you have traveled far in the System...have you never before encountered any of our kind? What sort of creatures inhabit the worlds?"

Curt suddenly knew what this Entity was getting at, what it wanted to know and *why*. Curt marshaled his thoughts and projected:

"Nowhere, until now, have we encountered the silicic life-form. On the moon of Neptune our scientists dis-covered purely gaseous entities in an advanced state of evolution, but they were not inimical to *us*. All life-forms elsewhere are protoplasmic." He felt this Entity probing deeply, hanging on his every thought. Grimly Curt went on.

He saw the degrees of civilization on Earth, Mars and Venus. The great cities and teeming populaces and scien-tific miracles. He dwelt on the savage and sun-hardened little tribes of Mercury, with their solar-powered cruisers. Earth's mighty armada passed in review through his mind. He pictured the terrible war that once raged between Mars and Earth, the hecatomb in space when weapons of every description had wrought havoc.

Curt finished at last. His mind went limp from the effort, but he felt he had done well.

The great crystal entity caught even that fleeting thought. The probing light intensified, and now it seemed amused.

"You come from the planet lying far to sunward, that called Earth. You have given me valuable information—which I would have taken from your mind anyway. You have shown me of your power, now I shall show you of ours."

The light tendrils clutched at his mind, tightened and throbbed painfully. Curt knew that Irene and Kraaz were feeling it too, as they went taut. Then—impression after pictured impression passed in review through his entranced mind.

They were passing through room after room in this underground world. The silicic populace numbered in the thousands. All were at work over furnaces and machines of strange design, turning out weapons such as Curt had never seen before. They saw some of these weapons in process of testing. The weapons lashed out with a power that wasn't electronic nor yet disintegrant—it seemed more than that.

These scenes faded, to be replaced by another. They saw hundreds upon hundreds of spacers, manned by the silicic creatures who stood ready near banks of strange and terrible weapons. The fleet swept upon Earth. Great cities were leveled and thousands died. Earth's battle fleet rose to meet them, only to be blasted out of existence in great whorls of radiant energy.

BUT something seemed wrong in this latter scene, and Curt exulted as he realized what it was. All of those hundreds of spacers had been based on the image of the *Astrogar*. At last these scenes faded...their minds were blank.

The great crystal-Entity seemed waiting, with a detached amusement. At last Curt dared to project his thoughts again:

"You've shown us only futuristic scenes, based on hopeful thinking. I say you're bluffing. You may have the weapons, yes—but where is the space fleet? You have none! You have no knowledge of space principles. Your civilization is trapped here and will die here..."

The great faceted pattern shifted angrily. Light rayed out so intense that Curt was sent staggering back.

"No spaceships? True, we have but one—and not enough metal for others. But with that one, we shall acquire more. And our civilization will not die here. It is the protoplasmic that will have to give way!"

"Fuel." Curt thought viciously. "You have no fuel to lift a ship from this gravity, and that's what has held you back this long."

"True." The thought came softly. "But you have provided that. I have read in your minds that another comes after you, following your trail. He comes in a powerful ship, with tremendous new propulsion drive. Perhaps we will utilize that ship, as well as our own..."

"Koerber," Curt breathed. The man was probably en route by now, and there could be no warning him. He would come stumbling in here, just as they had. And once the Entity gained Koerber's ship, the way to the other planets would be open for these silicic life forms.

Curt's mind was racing. They wouldn't strike directly at Earth—the Entity was too wary for that. No, they'd first take over Ceres Base where all those spacers were hidden. Next step would be a mass movement on the mines at Io or Callisto. They needed metal. The colonists would be wiped out—and that would be only the first step.

Kraaz must have been thinking the same thing. Without warning, he hurled himself forward. But fast as he was, the Entity was faster. It changed shape with a shifting the eye could hardly follow, and became a perfect blazing tetrahedron extending from the wall.

From the apex came a burst of light that caught Kraaz in mid-leap. It lifted him high. The light intensified, became a crackling angry red. For a full half minute Kraaz was held suspended, struggling and helpless, as his face twisted in pain and he tried to scream. Then with a contemptuous motion, the light tendrils flung him downward, stunned and bleeding.

Again the silicon-forms came forward. Tentacles reached out to grasp them, and they were led away.

CHAPTER SEVEN

THE hours were long, tedious. They sat in a gloomy stone cell, somewhere in the depths of the city. There was no doubt now that these creatures had weapons. On the way here they had passed several grottos where the strange radiant-energy weapons stood waiting and ready, with still others in process of manufacture. All these creatures needed were the spaceships—just *one* spaceship.

Kraaz paced the room angrily. He'd recovered, but was still nursing his wounds. Where that beam of light energy had touched, his flesh was covered with tiny red perforations that burned painfully.

"Let that be a lesson to you," Curt remarked. "You may be Jovian, but you're only protoplasmic."

Kraaz whirled angrily, then he grimaced and continued his pacing. "That iz right. I dezerve it. Iz my fault, all of thiz."

"We must stop Koerber somehow." Irene's voice bordered on panic. "If we could only get out of this dreadful place, and up to the surface. We might flash him a signal."

"Get out of here, with those animated rock piles patrolling the corridors?" Curt had tried it just a short while before, and received a ray treatment such as Kraaz had received. It was on a smaller scale, but enough to knock him almost senseless.

Shimmering light appeared just then in the open doorway, as one of the Silicytes paused there. It turned its blank faceted face toward them, scrutinizing.

Curt came to his feet, hurried toward the Silicyte guard. It raised a heavy arm, warningly. Light beamed out.

"Hold it, pal, hold it." Curt said nervously, slowing down. "I've already had one taste of that. All I want is to talk with you..."

The creature couldn't interpret sound, but it read Curt's thoughts. And it seemed curiously interested in the protoplasmic creatures. The crystalline arm lowered. Softer, intangible light came out to envelope Curt in an aura.

For several minutes Curt stood there in mental rapport with the guard, as Irene and Kraaz watched from the rear of the cell. Once they saw Curt fumble in his pockets, bring out bits of metal—a few coins, pocketknife, a chain of keys. These he tossed to the floor. The guard extended a crystalline tentacle, swept them up. The metal vanished in a glow of heat and energy. A slow roseate glow began to surge beneath the creature's translucent surface.

For another minute Curt spoke to it mentally, then the aura of light withdrew, the guard turned and lumbered away. Curt's expression was hopeless.

"Did you learn much?" Kraaz asked.

"NOTHING that'll do us any good. Believe me, these creatures all have a tremendous potential and they're dangerous, intelligent. That big crystalline pattern—the one that first spoke with us—is their leader, *the Silastah*. He's a super creation, the kingpin of—them all. He's grown through the years, incorporating other units into himself, only the highest scientific minds—it's hard to explain. He not only copes with the problem of survival, he has dreams of conquest. And all the others here are behind him, a hundred percent."

Irene was thoughtful. "What about those others we met up on the surface? Those black shapes?"

"I learned about them too," Curt shrugged. "They're only surface dwellers, and they have a reverent fear of the Silicytes because the Silicytes can control them mentally. It was the *'Silastah'* who flashed them the order to bring us here." Curt's face went grim. "And they'll get Koerber too, in the same way."

They were silent for a long while, wrestling with their problem.

"I have idea," Kraaz spoke. "Theze Zilicytes have had to burrow. *Metal* iz their lifeline, and it iz diminizhing. Curt...if you could bribe thiz guard..."

"Hell, I tried that. I told him I knew where there was lots of metal up on the surface. I even flashed him a picture of the wrecked *Astrogar.* They already know that. The word has gone out from *the Silastah* that the time is near, that they'll soon be leaving this world for new conquests."

They fell into a sleep of exhaustion, huddling on the bare stone floor. But it was a restless sleep. Pangs of hunger came. There was no food here, the only food the Silicytes knew was metallic.

They wakened, with hunger gnawing at them. Curt made swift calculation. Koerber should reach the asteroids from Ganymede in about forty hours, perhaps sooner if he had a new propulsion drive. If he left immediately after receiving Kraaz' code, that should bring him here sometime today.

A dozen times Curt paced angrily to the door, but the Silicyte guards were always there, watchful. Again he tried to converse with them, but now they remained uncommunicative. Curt hoisted the electro-gun thoughtfully. That was no good either. Already they'd learned that neither the electro nor the parala-ray was effective against these creatures. The Silicytes were so contemptuous of such weapons that they'd allowed the men to retain them.

Curt tried the electro against the cell walls. It soon became obvious there was no escape that way. This cell had been built into solid rock. He sank down in despair.

"Why do they keep uz here?" Kraaz wanted to know. "They have zome further uze for uz?"

"Yeah, I think they do. It's just a hunch, but I don't think these creatures have any knowledge of spaceships or space principles. But from what I've learned of their minds, they ought to pick that up pretty quickly."

IT WAS hours later when three guards came for them, flashing the thought: *Silastah summons you.*

"I'll give you ten to one," Curt muttered, "that Koerber's arrived and they've got him."

Once more they were led to the central grotto. But it was changed now. Many of the Silicytes were still there, retaining the roughly human shape—but they moved listlessly and they had gone dull. The *Silastah* was there. Curt could see its vast pattern sprawled across the far wall; it had dulled too, the faceted bulk of it lying there inert.

But it was alive and aware. Curt felt that. And with it, came a foreboding he couldn't explain.

And Curt had been right. Koerber was there. The man stood in the center of the grotto, staring around. He appeared at the same time bewildered and pleased.

"So it worked, just as I planned." Koerber said mockingly as they entered. "You found the *Astrogar,* and this asteroid as well. Your code came through perfectly, Kraaz. I picked up your trail at the Lanisar Group." He stared around at the listlessly moving Silicytes. "So Landreth was right. These creatures are really animated."

"Then you knew all the time what you'd find here." Curt exploded.

"No. Only partially. Landreth's impressions were wild and vague, even under the cerebro-scanner..."

Curt leaped forward, intent on smashing the man's grinning face. But Koerber was fast. A weapon appeared in his hand, he swung it around to cover them all.

"Your electro-gun, Vaughn. Toss it on the floor. And you, Kraaz…that parala-gun you're carrying. I can't trust *you* now, either."

They tossed their weapons down. Koerber shoved the guns with his feet, toward the Silicytes. Instantly several tentacles moved out, and the guns vanished in a roseate glow of heat.

"So that's the way they work," Koerber mused. "I suspected something like this, but I wasn't sure. Well, I can use them. They seem docile enough."

Docile. Yes, the Silicytes were being docile *now*. Curt's brain rioted, and he saw the whole plan. The *Silastah* hadn't communicated with Koerber at all. It realized it had a tool here in Koerber, and it was playing a cunning game.

"Koerber, what do you plan to do? I tell you these things are dangerous."

"Yes, they will be dangerous when I get through. I've seen how they go for metal, and how they propagate themselves by fission. Imagine what will happen when I turn a few hundreds of them loose at the mines on Io. And Callisto."

KRAAZ was staring at the man. "I am zorry I ever worked for you, Koerber. You are inzane."

"That may be. But I'll ruin the Earth Corporations, who own those mines. For years I've planned ways to get back at them, after what they did to me. Pirating in the spaceways hasn't been enough—but this should do the trick."

"Koerber, you're playing right into these creatures' hands. They're intelligent life forms, they're even telepathic. They have science and weapons and all they've been planning for years is to get away from this world, to achieve space-travel. Already the *Silastah* has listened to everything you've said."

"The *Silastah*...ah, yes, the word Landreth used." Koerber was smiling but he kept the weapon alert, covering them.

"Yes. It's the ruling Entity here and it's planning—" Curt stopped, realizing the futility. He whirled toward the expanse of wall where the *Silastah* sprawled. "That's it, there! Koerber, you imbecilic fool, it's reading your thoughts now, it knows what you plan to do..."

Koerber shrugged, glancing at the wall. "I see nothing there but a bunch of crystals. As for these other things," he glanced around, "anyone can see that they're merely low evolutionary crystal forms."

Curt faced the wall squarely, shouted: "You—the *Silastah!* Tell him. Show him everything you showed us."

There came no response beyond the barest thought-current. *The Silastah* was aware, and amused. Curt knew it. His shoulders slumped in despair.

"Enough of this," Koerber said.

"And now, my friends, you will help me. We ought to round up a hundred of these things for the first trip." He moved back a pace, waved his gun imperatively. "I mean it. Either you help or I'll blast you where you stand—all of you!"

Slowly they moved, herding together all the Silicytes in the place. There were perhaps a score of them here. Koerber remained watchful.

"That's enough for this time. We'll come back and find others—these caves seem to be endless."

The Silicytes moved forward, under prodding, toward the main tunnel leading out. They could have reached out with their radiant beams and blasted them all, but Curt knew they had no intention of doing that now—*not until they got aboard Koerber's ship and learned the controls.* The *Silastah* had informed them well.

Curt glanced back at the sprawled pattern of *the Silastah* and received a last faint impression, a mingled feeling of amusement and menace...and *purpose.*

CHAPTER EIGHT

WITH the lumbering Silicytes leading the way, they came out at last onto the asteroid's surface. Koerber came behind them, ever watchful. The way he handled that gun, they knew he wouldn't hesitate to blast them.

"At leazt thiz iz a break." Kraaz whispered, marching close to Curt. "We are out of that plaze."

"Too late now. There'll be no stopping those Silicytes."

"May be a way. If we can get to the zhip ahead of them. I zhall ztop Koerber anyway...I'll make a try for the gun."

"Not yet. Let him get closer." They glanced back at Koerber, who smiled twistedly and kept his distance.

"Watch those things up there," he called. "Don't let them spread out."

But there was no way the Silicytes could go now, except forward. They were struggling slightly upward through the narrow ravine. The footing was uncertain but Koerber, despite his handicap of only one good arm, scrambled after them like a gnarled mountain goat.

The way began to level out. Just ahead they could see the long sweep of the valley, an expanse of black sky. And then, they saw the wrecked *Astrogar* with another ship resting a short distance away—Koerber's ship, long and sleek and powerful. The Silicytes had seen it too. They were beginning to hurry ahead.

Curt glanced anxiously at Kraaz, saw him nod slightly.

"Tell Mizz Landreth to move away." Kraaz' voice was a whisper. Curt passed the word to her. She moved aside on the path as though looking for better footing.

Koerber was coming faster behind them now, having seen the Silicytes hurrying.

"Ztumble." Kraaz whispered. "Quickly!"

Curt didn't question him, but stumbled and went down, sideways. Kraaz bent as though to help him. His great muscles tensed as Koerber came on. Then he was hurling backward, toward Koerber's scrambling figure.

Koerber leaped aside, brought the gun up in a quick blast. The vibra-blast missed and went singing away. He didn't get a chance for another. Kraaz' tremendous bulk caught Koerber squarely in the middle, sent him spinning back. He crashed sickeningly against the rocky wall, slumped into a grotesque heap.

Kraaz pounced upon him, jerked him up with one hand while covering the gun with the other. Then he let Koerber fall again. "He'z dead. Skull iz cruzhed..."

A cry from Irene brought them whirling around. She was pointing wildly ahead, toward the Silicytes who hadn't even stopped.

But *one* of them had stopped, one of the rear stragglers. It had fallen prone. Now it was struggling desperately to rise but seemed unable to. It was literally falling apart.

"KOERBER'S blast did that!" Irene was crying. "I saw it!"

Curt whirled, snatched the gun from Kraaz. It was a strange weapon, with reinforced barrel and heavy firing coils.

"A Venusian vibratory gun. I've heard of them. Holy comets, Kraaz, this is it. The answer!"

"Anzwer?"

"The one way these Silicytes can be destroyed. The fact was staring at me all the time and I didn't realize it. Come on!"

They hurried to where the Silicyte lay, still struggling. Parts of it had already fallen away. It sensed them coming, tried to throw out the light rays to seize their minds. But it was a feeble light now.

Curt aimed the gun, felt a powerful recoil against his hand. The blast stashed across the Silicyte's form and back again. With a tinkling crash, a grinding of facet across facet, the thousands of crystals fell apart. At last it was over. They looked down upon a heap of dull, dead crystal.

"Lord knows what sort of cohesive power these things have," Curt exclaimed, "but a powerful vibratory rate disrupts it."

Most of the Silicytes had neared Koerber's ship by now, but three more of the stragglers had turned. They seemed to stare, as though suspecting something wrong. Then they came lumbering back toward the ravine.

"Trouble." Curt gritted, and balanced the gun in his hand. "Irene, you'd better get back, find a place to hide. I'll try to dispatch these three, before the others get wise."

They retreated deeper into the ravine, as the three Silicytes came toward them. The creatures paused for a moment where their dead companion lay; then, glittering angrily, they came on faster.

It had to be done quickly, Curt knew. He let them come close, waited until the light-tendrils reached out. Then he raised the gun in a snap shot. The blast caught the nearest one, sent it staggering back. A sort of shiver seemed to run the length of its body, but it came on. Again Curt blasted. It stumbled and fell, tried vainly to rise.

"One out of commission." Curt yelled, and shifted to the others. To his horror, he saw that they were both closing in upon Kraaz. He couldn't get them both. He trained his sight on the nearest one, held it there. The weapon's power seemed weaker now. Curt rushed in close. The second Silicyte went down with a splintering crash, thousands of crystals going dull as they fell away.

And now Kraaz was battling for his life. The remaining Silicyte had him in a relentless grasp, as glittering tentacles curved around him. Irene rushed in, pounded away at the creature with a rock, as Curt yelled for her to keep away. A lashing tentacle sent her sprawling. Curt circled quickly, trying to get a vantagepoint from which he could blast without injuring Kraaz.

THE Jovian's muscles bulged, but he was no match for cold, living crystal. Curt saw him going limp. He rushed close, and two more tentacles extended to grasp him, as tiny crystals slithered forward. Curt felt himself drawn close to the hard bulk of the creature. The breath was leaving him. Slowly he brought the vibra-blast around...released the firing stud.

The pressure slackened. One tentacle withdrew. Crystals were dropping away now, as the thing shuddered convulsively. Curt managed to shift the blast, and seconds later the Silicyte was crumbling about their feet. He stepped back and finished it off, did the same to the other two.

Kraaz' face was distorted in pain, but he said not a word. One arm was shredded and horribly burned, dangling limply. Curt knew Kraaz would never use that arm again.

The other Silicytes were gathered about the spacer, light flashing among them as if they were conversing. They seemed too excited to have missed their companions, or Koerber.

"Can't get them all with this gun." Curt said as they hurried forward. "But I have a plan that may work. We'll let them aboard...that's all they want anyway. Then I want you both to follow my instructions. Can you hold out, Kraaz?"

The Jovian nodded, gritting his teeth. He covered the injured arm with his tunic. Curt operated the lock, and the door swung down. Just as he had thought, the Silicytes permitted them to enter first.

"They want to watch us at the controls," Curt whispered hurriedly. "They'll learn everything they can about this ship—and they're intelligent. We must keep them busy, keep them interested. Five minutes should do it. Kraaz, you get back to the rocket feeds. Block those feeds, jam them tight, I don't care how you do it."

Kraaz nodded. Curt and Irene hurried forward, went to work. This was a wild chance, and if it didn't work they'd never have another.

The Silicytes were no longer the low-evolution types Koerber had thought them. Now they followed everywhere, watching the operations...intent...glittering with excitement Curt hurried to the control-console and checked it. He checked it again. He made minor adjustments. He switched on the V-Panel, and tested the magni-lens.

The creatures' thought-radiations touched his mind softly, inquiringly. Curt answered and felt their excitement.

They were on the threshold of a new experience, space travel.

But they were cautious too. Not yet suspicious, but cautious.

"These birds are technicians," Curt managed to whisper to Irene. *"The Silastah* must have selected them. They understand quickly." He moved over to the grav repulsors, tested them gently...He stepped to the navigator's table and began making adjustments of the blocking sheathes.

A THOUGHT radiation touched his mind, seized upon it fiercely. "No. We go first to that place you call...Ceres Base."

Curt shrugged, but went tight inside. Just as he'd thought, *the Silastah* had its mind set on all those pirate spacers hidden at Ceres. Curt made the adjustment. He glanced at the rocket-room door. If only Kraaz would hurry. He sensed a restlessness in these Silicytes now. If they were becoming suspicious...

Then Kraaz appeared, gave Curt a slight nod. Curt rose from the table, walked to the controls. He felt the Silicytes all around him, watchful. He set the control for major blast. He reached for the firing stud. Again, the radiations touched his mind, tenacious...definitely suspicious now. "We don't leave. We wait for *the Silastah.*"

It was now or never. Curt made his mind annoyed, projected the thought: *I'm only testing. We've got to test for rocket-blast.* His hand came down on the stud. With a rapid flick of the fingers he locked it into place.

He hoped Kraaz had blocked those feeds. There was no rocket roar. Only a vibration of the floor beneath their feet, of the very walls about them. In a split second it increased with a vicious surge, tearing at their nerves, wrenching at their limbs. The entire ship shuddered and threatened to fly apart.

Curt hurled himself back. He seized Irene and thrust her into the cushioned seat at the table. "Hold on! This'll be bad!"

Already the Silicytes were in distress. A few of them stood dazed. Others raced for the lock, stood there fumbling with the mechanism and then tumbled to the floor. The vibration increased, as the rocket-feeds held. The spacer shuddered and groaned under unleashed power.

Something gave way. The ship began spinning wildly across the asteroid rock in a vast pinwheel orbit. A few of the Silicytes had managed to reach the firing studs, and were fumbling at them, but it was too late now. In a matter of seconds they crumbled away into lifeless heaps of crystal.

Still the din continued, threatened to burst their ears. Curt felt as though every tissue were being shredded apart. The pinwheel spin was increasing now. Curt tried to reach the controls, but couldn't move. He felt himself blanking out.

HE STRUGGLED upward out of darkness, aware that the horrible din and vibration had ceased. His head ached unbearably. All about the ship lay heaps of dull crystal, literally thousands of insentient particles.

He saw Kraaz' pain-wracked face above him, and heard Irene sobbing hysterically. It was Kraaz who had managed to reach the controls, shut off the rocket blasts.

Curt came to his feet. With every move he made, it seemed as if a file were rasping across raw nerve ends.

"It's all right now," he comforted the girl. "It's all over. We'll be getting away from here fast!"

Kraaz gestured from the forward port. "Had better be fazt. Look out there!"

Curt peered, and his breath came out in a gasp. Across the asteroid's dark surface came row upon row of glittering shapes—more Silicytes, hundreds of them, advancing toward the ship. And leading them... Curt felt his mind reel.

It was *the Silastah* who led them, but a changed *Silastah* now. The super-Entity had taken on the form of a huge sphere, all of fifty feet in diameter. It rolled forward, glittering majestically—glittering proudly, as it felt victory within its grasp.

"Kraaz. Are those feeds okay? Any damage?"

"All ready. Zlight damage, but thiz zhip iz a marvel, it can take it."

Curt raced for the controls. Rockets roared, smoothly and rhythmically this time. The ship lifted gravs in a sweeping climb that skirted the asteroid cliffs.

"So they think they're going to Ceres. Not yet, they're not!" Through the panel Curt saw *the Silastah* race forward frantically, lift itself up in an angry scintillant movement. Curt exulted. They were beyond its reach now.

THEN he saw *the Silastah* pause, turn and roll toward the wrecked *Astrogar*.

"Oh, no. You don't get that ship either! You might be able to repair it." Curt brought their ship around in a swift arc of rocket-fire. He came low across the *Astrogar*, giving it blast after blast from the forward tubes. At last, the *Astrogar* went up in a shuddering explosion of tangled wreckage.

"We'll get more vibra-blasts," Curt said grimly. "Huge ones, improved ones. We can come back and blast this hunk of rock out of space, and *the Silastah* with it. I won't feel safe until then."

Irene shuddered, watching the dark world drop away. "If only the Earth officials will believe us—"

Curt grinned, reached to an inside pocket and brought out his compact camera. "They'll believe now. I had this set on automatic speed control. I took enough pictures back there to convince anyone."

Kraaz was at the first-aid cabinet, applying unguents to his shredded arm. Curt turned to Irene.

"There's only one thing bothering me. You're still half Ganymedian. The dark skin, how'd you ever manage that?"

"Special treatment, under the Ulmo-lamps. And," her eyes sparkled, "they tell me it doesn't wear off, inside of a year."

Curt sighed. "I can't wait *that* long, now can I? Besides I kind of like you this way. Come here."

He took her into his arms.

THE END

www.ingramcontent.com/pod-product-compliance
Lightning Source LLC
Chambersburg PA
CBHW030328180626
46810CB00003B/1267